THE EXTRAS

ALSO BY WAYNE KARLIN

Lost Armies
Crossover

Wayne Karlin

THE

EXTRAS

HENRY HOLT AND COMPANY   NEW YORK

PUBLISHED BY HENRY HOLT AND COMPANY, INC.,
115 WEST 18TH STREET, NEW YORK, NEW YORK 10011.
PUBLISHED IN CANADA BY FITZHENRY & WHITESIDE LIMITED,
195 ALLSTATE PARKWAY, MARKHAM, ONTARIO L3R 4T8.

LIBRARY OF CONGRESS CATALOGING-IN-PUBLICATION DATA
KARLIN, WAYNE.
THE EXTRAS / WAYNE KARLIN.—1ST ED.
P. CM.
ISBN 0-8050-1076-9
I. TITLE.
PS3561.A625E97   1989
813'.54—DC19   89-1758
                                                     CIP

HENRY HOLT BOOKS ARE AVAILABLE AT SPECIAL DISCOUNTS
FOR BULK PURCHASES FOR SALES PROMOTIONS, PREMIUMS,
FUND-RAISING, OR EDUCATIONAL USE. SPECIAL EDITIONS
OR BOOK EXCERPTS CAN ALSO BE CREATED TO SPECIFICATION.

FOR DETAILS CONTACT:
SPECIAL SALES DIRECTOR
HENRY HOLT AND COMPANY, INC.
115 WEST 18TH STREET
NEW YORK, NEW YORK 10011

FIRST EDITION

Book Design by Claire M. Naylon
PRINTED IN THE UNITED STATES OF AMERICA
1   3   5   7   9   10   8   6   4   2

A portion of this book previously appeared in New Outlook,
January 1976.

· · · · · · · · · · · ·

As always, to Ohnmar and Adam, for putting up with me.

With special thanks

to Meir, my reader, for his invaluable help and patience

to Basil, who's been there from the beginning

to Salah, for making my house his and his house mine

to Tracy, for believing in it

to Dan, Laura, Lisa, Lynea, and Michael,
for their helpful suggestions

to Moshe, who I hope will understand
the love that went into it

to my friends and family in *ha'aretz,*
with love and with hope.

PART ONE

. . . . EZRA

A rotted cardboard suitcase, open like a book, haunted the front gate of the refugee camp. I swerved to avoid running over it. Inside, staggered rows of mud huts crumbled around eye-socket windows. I parked next to a long whitewashed building with jalousie blinds in its windows and a UNRRA sign over its front door. I had no idea where to look.

The square in front of the building was packed with people, cameras on tripods, klieg lights, and microphones sticking up here and there from them like the banners of the army of technology. Bashir had told me that the camp was being used to represent the Jewish slave quarters in the Land of Goshen. The mob was made up of men dressed uniformly in frayed sports jackets over work clothes, keffiyeh headdresses or knit ski caps on their heads, scuffed, heavy-toed work shoes on their feet—Arab day laborers from the camp or nearby, vying to become Children of Israel. They'd earn more in a day working as extras than they'd earn in a week working over the Green Line.

Bashir came out of the UNRRA building. He was wearing a red shirt, jeans, and a leather cowboy hat. He began to wade into the mob, cursing loudly in Arabic, grabbing men by their shoulders and trying to shove them into a line. As soon as he saw me, he stopped, then walked over, his eyes shining.

"Ezra, *ahalahn*. I'm glad you could make it."

I could barely hear him above the noise. He took my elbow and leaned in close to my ear. "I have a surprise for you." He was grinning like a boy.

We skirted the edge of the mob, around to a padlocked gate in a low stone wall that surrounded three stone huts. As Bashir fumbled in his pocket for the key, I saw a tall, magnificently bearded figure in a snow white keffiyeh and a flowing abayah robe edged with gold embroidery come striding toward us like a character from the wrong movie.

Bashir bowed with a flourish, flashing a conspiratorial smile at me. The man began speaking in a gunfire-rapid Arabic that I could barely follow. Apparently he really was a Bedouin sheikh and not an actor. He'd heard that when the Americans were filming in the Negev, the Bedouin had received only half of what the other extras were getting. A lie, Bashir said. And the animals, the sheikh went on, as if Bashir hadn't spoken. Men furnishing and working with their animals should receive a double measure. That should be understood.

"Trust me," Bashir said.

We watched the sheikh walk majestically away.

"Bashir the *macher*," I said.

He glanced at me brightly, assessing. A slight frown twitched his face: I'd promised sobriety, but it hadn't worked out.

"I hired his tribe right out of the Sinai," he said. "Camels, donkeys, blue tattoos, veiled women who look like they want to cut off your business and ululate. They're to be Amalekites. All I need to do is keep them away from the Jericho Arabs I hired—they hate each other's guts. Nomads and dwellers in the cities. Nothing changes." He clapped my shoulder. "I'm a magician, Ezra, not a *macher*. The magic Druze. I separate warring tribes, turn Arabs into Jews." He waved at the mob. The men were pushing toward a gap directly opposite the gate we stood before, on the other side of the low stone wall. The gap funneled them into a single file, which disappeared into the black doorway of one of the huts. On the other side, they emerged clad in gray and ocher-colored robes, transformed.

"But are you happy in your work?"

Bashir sighed. "Last year, for *Jesus,* I hired some Moroccan porters for the set work. One of them, Eli Cabillo—do you know him?—I asked how he, a Jew, felt about carrying that big cross around. 'Jesus, refrigerators, it's all the same to me,' he said."

The noise of the mob increased, blended to a single, collective wail of protest.

"I don't know what the hell I'm doing here," I said.

"Oh, I'm the last circle of hell, *habibi.* I'm who you gravitate to, on your way down."

"Where are we going with this, Bashir?"

He smiled mysteriously, enjoying being the *macher,* the arranger. "Come on, I have something for you. Someone I want you to meet."

He opened the gate and pointed to one of the huts inside, next to the one where the potential extras were being signed up.

"Quickly, Ezra. A pity on the time."

Going inside was like entering a cool, gloomy cave, its darkness split by the beams of light coming through the single, reed-latticed window. There were piles of gray and rust-colored cloths against one of the walls, and a row of prop spears leaning on another. A woman was standing in the middle of the floor. The sight of her, costumed in a long, off-white cotton robe, her face half-hidden by its hood, sent a heavy rolling shock through me in spite of its theatricality. She moved, perhaps deliberately, so that a bar of light illuminated her face. Her skin was copper colored, her eyes green and startling against it in the light. Her face eluded me. I wasn't even sure if she was Jewish or Arab, and with that thought I knew who she was.

"It's good to see you again, Ezra," Maryam Halim said.

She smiled briefly, then quickly turned it into a frown, as if she felt that was the more appropriate expression. I couldn't stop staring at her, watching the girl I'd known—a small, skinny child and then a reedy adolescent—growing older, her breasts and hips swelling under the cotton as though by some movie trick. Unbidden images of the games we'd played, games of slow, delicious discovery, formed in my mind. Maryam closed her eyes suddenly, tightly, as if she'd shared the memory and was shutting it out, grinding it out.

When I was a boy, I'd imagine Maryam a princess held captive in the stone castle of her house, the castle of a cruel sheikh. Her father, Walid, fit the physical image—he had the debauched look of a Semitic despot—but he was really a rather kindly man, and the castle, the Halims' house, had actually been given to him, for services rendered, by the YMCA: Walid Halim was a poet who for years made his living as head clerk of that institution. His house was across the street from it, at the end of the alley between the French Consulate and the King David Hotel; it stood on the ridge just above the old border, its rear windows bricked against sniper fire. Before independence, my father had cultivated Walid's friendship, and my uncle, as a young Irgunist, had warned Walid of the attack on the King David, telling him to keep his windows open and stay inside: an act that may have saved the lives of Walid and his wife, Aida, and that certainly held down the amount of damage to the house.

Whenever I'd visit (our apartment was nearby), I'd be shown the crack in the living-room wall from the King David blast, as if to establish my familial connection. Then Maryam, her twin brother, Shahid, and I would go up to the roof and peek through the crenellations of its walls at the echoing crenellated wall of the city across the valley and the terraced hills around it from which their father had separated them when he'd decided to keep the house and stay on the Jewish side of the city in 1948. A nationalist, he wrote that the only chance the Palestinian Arabs had for survival lay in living with and outbreeding the Jews. A pan-Arabist, a Moslem, he'd married a Christian girl from Ein Kerem. His children were Arabs to the Jews, Christians to the Moslems, Moslems to the Christians. When we were both fourteen, Shahid and I played in a citywide youth soccer league, and most of our teammates were Kurdish Jews from the Katamon neighborhood. We came onto the YMCA field, Walid and Maryam watching from a balcony in the building behind the stands—Aida always refused to come—and the crowd would chant, "Kill the Arab."

It was on the roof of their house, staring at the Old City and at the coils of barbed wire and the valley that divided me from it, as from my own friends, sensing for the first time the connections between buildings and landscape and my own life, that I first wanted to be an architect, that I had the illusion I could impose my own shapes on the world.

I'd lost touch with the Halims when I turned eighteen and went for my army service, though in 1967, fighting through the streets of the Old City, the audience I pictured watching me was Maryam and Shahid, observing me from their roof, praying for my safety, praying for my death. A week after the war, instead of going with my buddies to the Wall we'd conquered, I went to the Halims' house, as if it were my own shrine. Still half battle crazy, still drunk with the giddy goodwill of reunification, I imagined the three of us standing together on the roof like a propaganda poster, looking across at the border between us that I'd helped erase, at the valley between us that I'd helped clear of its barbed wire and mines. But the house had been abandoned, emptied. Later I found out from my uncle that Shahid had indeed gone to the roof, to watch the war like a movie, and had been killed by a sniper's bullet—no one knew from which side. As soon as the cease-fire had come into effect, the Halims had left, Walid taking them to the newly liberated/occupied West Bank, to Jebel Halim, the village from which his family came. He'd died there a year later of cancer of the liver, of grief, of bad decisions.

Maryam was looking at me curiously.

"I'm sorry about your father. And Shahid," I said lamely.

She nodded. "I'm sorry also—I heard about Amos. I liked him very much."

We stood in an uneasy silence, too many new valleys, new borders, between us. Bashir stared at us, the look of expectation dying slowly on his face. "Come on, Ezra, let's get you dressed," he said, his voice suddenly harsh. He was a romantic and our awkward reunion had disappointed him.

Maryam went out and Bashir helped me with the costume: a robe made of a single swath of gray cotton, belted with a sash at the waist, a gray keffiyehlike cloth over my head, more cloth wrapped bandagelike around my feet and ankles for sandals. I walked outside, feeling like a fool.

Maryam was waiting in the street. "The sheikh of Araby," she said. She didn't smile.

We followed Bashir down the main street of the camp, a rubble- and trash-strewn path bordered by open sewers. It ended at a bisecting cross street. At one corner was a high courtyard wall that had broken glass embedded in its rounded top. A technician was straddling it, methodically breaking off the teeth of glass in front of him with a small hammer as he inched along. Other technicians were laying tracks along the street for the cameras.

"Wait here," Bashir said. "You two will be my gathering point. I'll be back in a few minutes."

"And then what do we do?" Maryam asked. "When you're back?"

"Walk out of Egypt."

We sat down with our backs against the courtyard wall. "I'm surprised your mother let you work here," I said.

Maryam tossed her head. "Then you don't remember Aida very well—do you picture her as a veiled primitive?"

There wasn't anything I could say that wouldn't offend her. I needed a drink. There was a half-full bottle of cognac under my front seat; I cursed myself for leaving it.

"No, of course not," I said.

"Why are you here?"

"Bashir needed bodies and I needed the money. I'm a poor student."

She grinned, as if remembering. "Architecture?"

"Yes," I said, and the lie ached like an old wound.

"Where?"

"I commute to the Technion," I said, and I wondered what kind of lie it was when you put your good intentions into words.

She looked at me curiously. "I would have thought you had your degree already."

I shrugged. "There were interruptions."

She stared off into the street. She knew what the interruptions were and refused to acknowledge them.

"Tell me what you've been doing," I said.

"I'm starting at Givat Ram, in the spring."

I grinned back at her. "Literature?"

Her gaze flitted away from mine again, away from the ties we'd had, the long, earnest conversations about our futures we'd engaged in as adolescents.

"I'm in the graduate program," she said. "I studied in the States."

"How was that?"

"Like being in a film." She plucked at the sleeve of her robe. "In America you put on a different identity merely by putting on a different costume."

"Is that why you came here—do you like putting on costumes?"

She turned and regarded me coolly. "Yes. For a little while I can be somebody else. A different cliché. Some other cliché than a terrorist or a veiled primitive. It's a vacation, like being outside the country again. On my way back from America, I traveled in Europe . . ."

"I was there."

"Yes? Where?"

"All over." I named the interruption she hadn't wanted to hear about. "After the last war, I spent a year just wandering around. France and Italy mostly, but then I studied in Germany for a while."

She nodded. "Germany. Then you understand what I mean. When I was in Scandinavia, I told people I was an Arab, a Palestinian; when I was in Germany I told them I was a Jew."

"What do you want to be in real life?"

"Swiss."

The rest of the afternoon we were marched over and then over again down the center path of the camp: the two of us walking in front of a drooling camel and the crowd pressing behind and around us; the people I'd seen pushing for jobs that morning now carried prop bundles and balanced prop baskets on their head, doing the Exodus. The bright light of the day burned into our eyes in hard, painful waves off the white walls of the huts, so that we seemed to be moving through a tunnel, its sides blurred with light.

We were marched to the end of the street and then sent back to do it again. Each time something went wrong. Too much dust. The shadow and wind from a watching army helicopter. An Israelite with scuffed work shoes sticking out from beneath his robe. Besides the men, Bashir had hired a sprinkling of American and European women, tourists or students he'd lured to the desert with tales of the movies—Maryam was the only Arab woman I saw there. The foreign women had been given young camp boys, as prop children, I suppose, and the boys—twelve- and thirteen-year-olds with the faces of men and the physiques of seven- or eight-year-olds—pinched the women's bottoms and breasts until one American screamed and punched a boy in the mouth and then screamed again when he punched her back. We were called back to do the march again. The film crew grew impatient. They cursed at us and talked loudly about us, as if we weren't there. The Arabs mimicked them to get back. It was the whispered, satiric humor of slaves.

At the end of the street was a hut whose front wall had been demolished in some more recent historic event, though it had happened long enough ago that the inner walls had had time to weather evenly with the outer and there wasn't the startled, obscene sense of exposure you usually experience with such places. In one inside corner were some black and twisted fingers of dung, a halo of flies around them. We were marched forward and called back, flowing in reverse past the hut again. I focused on it, redesigning and rebuilding it in my mind: picturing the dung disappearing and the front wall re-forming, row after row of bricks leaping on one another when the film ran backward, and then quickly being covered by a layer of clean, white clay.

The spotlights switched on, intensifying the already intense light of the day. The crowd, we, stared stonily at the film crew, a bitter odor of sweat on us. I narrowed my eyes and fluttered us forward, picturing us gliding, through the magic of film, past the cameras and equipment and past the border of the camp and spilling into the desert with our camels and donkeys and possessions.

. . . . M A R Y A M

Jerusalem at night was a wild marketplace crowd turned into
stone by a magician: buildings pushing against each other,
leaning, arguing with silently flowing shadows.

A cat, its back hunched with wariness, licked at a puddle
in front of a shuttered shop and kept its eyes on me as I went
past.

I felt childish. The little game Riad wanted me to play
seemed just that—a little game, not unlike the hide-and-seek
I'd played near this same place when I was a girl. Move
through their streets, he'd said. See if you're stopped. When
I was a girl, the Arabic we spoke at home became hopelessly
twisted and melded into the Hebrew we spoke on the streets
and in school; the words and cadences of the language finally
seeped into my bones and blood, into the very movements
of my body. Go among them again, Riad had said, drawing
cabalistic patterns on the city map he'd laid out on the table.
Let's see how you do it.

I walked to Karen Kayemet, then up to King George.
The street was nearly empty, but well lit. I let the light play

on my face. Look. My shadow lengthened, repossessing the street as I walked. I extinguished it in the swallowing, peaceful darkness of Independence Park.

I emerged from the park across the street from the American Consulate, crossed the street, and went down the alley that ran through to the YMCA soccer field. The walls of the alley were interrupted by the round openings of drainage pipes, little mouths gaped open in stupid surprise to see me again. The pipes were at staggered heights: the ninth was nearly at my waist level. I felt inside it until my fingers touched something. A crumpled cigarette packet. I put it into my purse.

No one has followed me, Riad. No one has stopped me. Do you see?

On King David, I caught a bus to the center of town and then a number 12 bus to East Jerusalem. The couple across the aisle from me were talking about the wave of bombings in the city. "Someone just needs the balls to shoot a few of our cousins," the man said. He saw me staring at him and smiled at me, as if he knew who I was. A cousin. The woman with him turned and smiled also. Their heads exploded, their smiling lips melted, shriveled like burning worms, smoke poured from the holes of their eyes and nostrils. I closed my eyes, canceling the vision. Against my palms I felt the vibration of the bus through the cold metal of the seat rail; it made me realize how tightly I was gripping it. The bus shuddered and stopped. I heard the pneumatic hiss of the brakes. Silence.

I opened my eyes. The two were still staring at me, curiously now. The woman had a small, hard face that her smile didn't soften. There was a slamming noise, a shout, and then the faces truly flared into two blurs of intense light, as if my wishes had at last become weapons.

But the light was coming from outside, shining through the windows.

Flashlights, I told myself.

"Get the hell off the bus," someone yelled.

The Jew who had been staring at me rose and grabbed my shoulder. I let him push me, toward the resting place of a cell.

"The fucking Arabs," he said.

He shoved me outside, into the center of a circle of lights; their beams pinned me like an insect. Soldiers were screaming at me. A man came forward, walking behind a camera as if it were slowly pulling him. I slapped at the lens and he wove out of my way. Soldiers were inside the floodlit bus, looking under the seats. I stepped into a dark, muttering crowd of onlookers. The intense light was seeping back out through the windows and cracks of the bus as if it were spilling fire: a preview of how it would look if the bomb exploded. I backed off into the crowd and then walked away. No one cared.

At Damascus Gate, a tall, thin man in a blue pin-striped suit gave me an oily smile. "Do you have any dollars to change, madame?"

He'd spoken in English. I answered in Arabic.

"I'm sorry, you're mistaken. I'm not a tourist."

I followed him. Past the bus station, the spotlighted skull of the Protestant Golgotha grinning down at me. Left on Salah-a-din. How could he walk in front of me and tell if anyone was following us? The man patted the side of a doorway as he went past. It was to the restaurant where I'd met Riad before.

I went up a flight of stairs, up to the cartoon palace of

my dreams. The decor of the place had enchanted me when I was thirteen and first saw it, offended me by the time I was fourteen and forever after. Rudolph Valentino Arab, Aida had called it. Tourist Arab, and even that worn at the edges: frayed cushions instead of chairs, low tables, tarnished brass trays and lamps, stained wall tapestries, dusty alcoves behind beaded curtains. It's perfect, Riad had said the first time he'd met me here—who would take this place seriously?

He sat in the same booth now, smoking a cigarette gripped in a theatrically long holder, as if he were physically satirizing the setting.

"Ah, Maryam. Sit. Would you like some coffee?"

"No."

"Drink something. Else why be in a restaurant?"

It was a command. He waved the cigarette holder and a magic waiter appeared and brought me coffee on a golden tray.

"Thank you," Riad said, taking the cigarette pack from my hand under the table. I wondered if it contained anything, any message, or if it was just part of the game, the test. "And thank you for coming. Were there any problems?"

"One of your bombs nearly killed me."

"There was nothing on that bus, Maryam. The soldiers stopped it and searched it because of a telephone threat."

I felt a rise of anger as the meaning of his words focused in my mind.

"Are you all right?"

"Yes."

"You had no difficulty otherwise?"

"No."

Riad smiled, choosing to ignore the curtness of my answers. "If I'd gone through the areas you went through, I would have been stopped ten times. If I'd been on that bus, I would have been arrested."

"You called the police, you bastard."

Riad arched his eyebrows lazily. "Of course."

"What's the point of it? What's the point of all this walking in circles, Riad?"

He took a tiny sip of his coffee. "Suppose you tell me. Suppose, let's say"—he considered the cup gravely, rocking the coffee back and forth in it—"suppose, instead of walking in circles, I'd asked you to leave something behind for me on that bus. Would you be willing to do that?" He finished the coffee, then held the cup between his thumb and forefinger, peering into it as if to see the future.

The cup had left a wet ring on the table. I streaked it across the Formica with my fingers.

"I've told you—it's just that I'm not ready, Riad," I said.

"And when will you be ready?"

"I don't know if I can hurt anyone."

He nodded. "Then what you'll do is walk in circles." We both looked down at my hand on the tabletop. Describing circles.

He put down his cup. "How was it today—did Bashir arrange your meeting?"

"Riad, does he work for you?"

"Bashir works for anyone. One day I may kill him, when he's no longer useful. Was he useful today, Maryam?"

I looked down at the table. "Yes. But I still don't understand why you wanted me to see Ezra Brenner again."

"He's associated with Deddy Gur. With the Breira group."

He smiled as if the reason were self-evident. I shrugged.

"It's a group we're interested in," he said.

"In what way—speaking to them?"

His smile widened.

"Breira is progressive, a peace group," I said.

"A Zionist peace group. Don't you find that something of a contradiction in terms, Maryam? Like Israeli-Arab?"

Riad reached over and stopped the nervous motion of my hand.

"I'm just giving you what you wanted," he said. "A chance to help us without hurting anyone."

. . . . EZRA

I was walking down Ben Yehuda when the police car parked
at the bottom of the street exploded. There was a blossom
of orange-red flame and then a thick gray exclamation mark
of smoke billowed up from the remains of the chassis. For a
second I felt caught up in some hugely malicious practical
joke. My ears were ringing, though I had no memory of
hearing the explosion. Time seemed to be stretching, with
details and sensations coming only slowly into focus: the
spasmed crouch I'd assumed, the familiar stench of kerosene
and cordite, the pedestrians lying facedown around me on
the sidewalk. One of them raised his head at me and gasped,
"Get down, man." But already several policemen and passersby were grasping hands and trying to form a cordon
around the wreckage. A siren wailed. The people lying down
near me began picking themselves up and moving away, like
players who'd received a cue.

I straightened up and walked to the cordon. A large, red-
faced man with a stricken expression twisting his features

came walking up the street toward me, wringing his hands. I stared at him; I'd never seen anyone literally wringing his hands before. The man was twisting them like a dish towel.

"The fucking Arabs," he said.

By the time I reached the car, Zion Square was crowded with police, soldiers, spectators. The police had already started to block off the square with sawhorses. People were talking to one another angrily, looking around in frustration for an enemy at whom to strike. There was a sudden burst of movement near Zion Cinema and I saw two Arabs, each carrying a plastic shopping basket and dressed identically in white keffiyehs, frayed gray jackets, and baggy tan pants, break from the knotted crowd and begin running east on Jaffa. The burly man who sold lotto tickets in front of the cinema reached out and grabbed the handle of one of the baskets, and the Arab it belonged to swung back to him in an arc, like an object that had reached the end of its string. For a moment the two men engaged in a cartoon tug-of-war, until the plastic handle broke and the contents of the bag—tomatoes, oranges, cartons of cigarettes—spilled into the gutter. There was a quick, vicious flurry of fists around the Arab as the crowd closed in, and then a wedge of helmeted policemen charged, swinging clubs. A few seconds later the lotto dealer was sitting on the curb, holding his head in his hands, and the two Arabs had joined the line of other Arabs being filed into a police van on the other side of the square. I scanned the line, but I saw no faces I knew.

There was no going back up Ben Yehuda. I pushed my way through to Jaffa, walked west to King George, and went up that street until it joined with Ben Yehuda again. The Gallery Café had emptied: the few customers who'd been in it at this hour of the morning were clustered in front of the doorway, talking animatedly about the bombing. I went inside and sat at one of the small tables lining the wall. Nissim, the owner, hadn't moved from behind the counter; he was wiping glasses with a towel, displaying the stolid sense of detachment he seemed built around—a militant indifference to the world outside the café. Without a word, he brought me a small cup of Turkish coffee and a sweet roll.

The long room of the café was filled with gauzy yellow light; the photographs hung on the walls had become Rorschach puzzles, gray and white blurs. The coffee steamed in front of me; the cold air intruding through the open front door was laced with its fresh chicory smell and with the warm, spicy odor of the newly baked cakes and rolls in the display rack behind the front window. The smells and the light and the early morning feel were normal and comforting and I tried to concentrate on them.

I finished the coffee and Nissim came over to take the cup. He stared at me.

"Can I get you anything else?"

"A sense of detachment."

"I'll bring a cognac," Nissim said.

When he did, I drank it. It worked on the thick knot in my stomach. Nissim had the radio on. There had been two policemen in the car. A passerby had noticed a milk canister left in the doorway of a shop off Zion Square and had waved them over. The policemen had decided to move the canister immediately before the square got crowded, rather than wait for the bomb squad.

When I looked up from my glass, I saw Maryam standing in the door of the café. I waved to her and she walked back to the table. Her eyes were bright with wariness.

"I was worried about you," I said. "The police are picking up people in Zion Square."

She shrugged. "I'm usually taken for Jewish."

She sat with her back to the wall. Her skin took the yellow light of the café into copper shades, that startling green of her eyes against the copper. She looked Jewish, yet didn't. I searched her face for the similarities and differences of our flesh. There was a worry line between her eyes, a groove cut into the memory photograph of the girl I'd known. I wanted to reach across and smooth it away. She smiled at me, mocking my stare. I waved to Nissim.

"What are you drinking?" she asked me.

"Cognac."

"I'll just have coffee."

Nissim nodded and brought over a cup. She poured sugar into the already sweet, thick mixture and stirred it slowly, peering into the cup.

"I *was* stopped," she said. "Harassed a little, then told to run along, like a naughty child. That seems to be the only time we're noticed—when we make loud bangs, like a child who's been ignored. Then everybody suddenly knows that we're here."

I could still see a small, bright afterimage of the exploding car, a flamed moth on the periphery of my consciousness, a visual, pursuing echo from my own past.

"You don't know what you're talking about," I said.

We sat without speaking, the bombing sitting heavily with us, like a stranger at the table. I raised my glass. "To reunions," I said.

Maryam looked at me, startled, and laughed.

"I thought I saw you at the university, when I went to register," she said. "At a Breira rally with Deddy Gur? He asked why Israel shouldn't negotiate with the PLO and someone answered him by throwing a Molotov cocktail at the podium. Someone who wanted to be noticed."

I took a pack of cigarettes from my shirt pocket and offered it to her. She drew one out gingerly, as if fearing a trap. I lit it for her, the flare of the match a brief shock that startled both of us into smiles.

"Maybe I'd like to talk to Gur sometime," she said. "Can you arrange that?"

"Sure," I said. "Deddy is always looking for Arabs to talk to."

She drew in on the cigarette, exhaled with a sigh. "You make it sound like being a guest at one of your father's brotherhood dinners. Arabs and Jews and cakes and grapefruit juice."

"Something like that."

"Is that what Breira is? A way for people like you and Deddy Gur to feel good about yourselves? A liberal game?"

"Maybe it is." I was getting more than a little bored with the conversation. "Do you remember some of the other kinds of games we used to play, Maryam—when we were children and wanted to be noticed? The games we'd play in the Jerusalem forest, or upstairs, when your brother was away?"

She grinned, surprising me. "I remember—but don't make too much of that. All children are curious. And it was a long time ago."

"Not that long."

We stared at each other, then Maryam's eyes crinkled with an amusement that I understood immediately, and I had to smile too. In each other we would always see children playing games, playing at the conversations and actions of adults. Playing at Arabs and Jews. For an instant I saw the girl I'd known develop like a photograph over the woman. She put her hand on my arm, reaching over the little space between us. And took it away quickly. Her touch stayed on my skin like an echo of heat.

"Today you're a star," the blond said, smiling at her.

The parody shrugged, pleased. "It's just a small walk-on, a few words. I'm to be a whore for Moses."

When they'd finished, they pushed me out of the tent, into the bright light of the world. I felt silly in the robe. We were shooting in the desert outside the camp. The hills rose around us like what? White elephants? More like a peeled brain. A group of Jericho Arabs—six boys, students hired by Bashir—were sitting in a circle around a small fire they'd built next to one of the trucks. They were brewing coffee in a small finjan, self-conscious about their costumes and the picture they were making around the fire, in the desert— Arabs trying to look like Arabs.

One of them, a redhead, saw me staring and grinned. "Come sit," he said, in English, to my relief. His friends laughed softly, embarrassed. He edged over and patted the space next to him. I sat down. The boys looked surprised and uneasy: they hadn't really expected me to take up his offer. They were nice boys really, but if they knew I was Arab, they'd take me for a whore. A whore for Moses. As a foreigner my forwardness could be excused as coming from ignorance.

We sat and watched the coffee bubble thickly in the small cylinder of the finjan, the heat from the fire on my front and the sun baking my back, two different heats that sent chills through me, the way drinking coffee on a hot day does. A Bedouin trick. The Bedouin were singing, their chanting coming from some unknown point or points farther out in the desert. The redhead passed me a cup, took off his movie headdress, and used it to grab the handle of the finjan. Our costumes made everything—the fire, the small, long-handled pot, the distant chanting, the desert itself—into props.

The redhead poured coffee for me, then the others. And

. . . . M ARYAM

But he didn't come back to the film the next day. I was
relieved. He wasn't there, Riad, what could I do?

Two women waited for me in the shadows of the cos-
tuming tent: one young and dark, the other middle-age and
blond. The blond, an Italian, had square, mannish shoulders
and moved with a jerky energy. The younger woman, Israeli, seemed to have taken on the gestures and movements
of her boss. She followed her around the tent like a parody.

"*Bene!*" the blond called to me, flinging her arms apart
and bringing them together with a great clap. "*Nudi, nudi,*"
the Israeli said, making the same movement. They both pantomimed undressing with exaggerated gestures; they wanted
me to strip and sit and be transformed into a parody also. I
stripped to my underwear. They dressed me. The parody
leaned close to my face, plucking at my eyebrows. She was
made up herself, her eyelids covered with thick amber paste,
the shape of her eyes outlined and elongated with kohl, her
eyebrows joined into a single black line. I let her do what
she wanted.

maybe I was wrong about them too. I knew that in many of the West Bank colleges these days men and women went to classes together and were progressive about the relationship between the sexes. The phrase "relationship between the sexes" echoed in my mind, sending a different chill through me, a shiver from the grave: it was the kind of pompous language my father would use. The redhead smiled at me slyly, as if he'd read my thoughts.

"It's good, yes? Good Arab coffee. You like it?"

"Yes, yes, it's very good." *Berry gut.* I fought down a rise of contempt. Oily grins, leers, the whole Arab sex act: our costumes that turned us into props and parodies.

"Where you from? Here?"

The others smiled and winked at one another, listening to their friend chat me up in English.

"No."

"America?" *Ameereekah.*

"No. Mexico."

A blank look. Total incomprehension. "Mexico?" *Mezzicho.*

"Yes. Acapulco."

The boy regarded me, something glinting in his eye. "Very good, then. Mexico. We are from Jericho. But now we are all here, we are all film actors, no? Do you like the work here? No? The money is good, money for nonsense, everybody says that. But we like to be in a karate film. You know karate?" He chopped the air.

"No."

"No? No karate in Mexico, is it?"

"We study," a slim dark boy said earnestly to me.

"Karate?"

"Yes. In a school. A special school."

Beshul skull.

"A weapon for the weaponless," the redhead said, as if my father had coaxed his syntax. He smiled at me in conspiracy.

"Our school is in Jericho," he said. "You should come there. I show you the city. It's beautiful. An oasis."

Ohahzizz.

"So I've heard."

"Good, by God you'll come."

The Bedouin chanting drifted to us again. The boys turned to look.

"Ha," the slim dark boy said, like a word.

One of the others produced a small skin drum from his robe, like a magic trick, and the boys all grinned tightly at each other. The slim boy ran the top of the drum over the fire, in a circular movement. He took it back, tapped the skin a few times to judge its tightness, then began beating it. The others sang, the redhead leading. The Bedouin chanting flowed between his verses and their responses like dissonant echoes. The redhead was improvising jokes around his friends' names. The Bedouin singing grew louder and he picked up his voice, and so did the others, the singing battling back and forth. The redhead began to parody the Bedouin *gasidah,* mocking, placing perverts and hunchbacks and whores into the endless noble begatting of the Bedouin. It was crazy and he'd get us killed, but he made me smile. He looked at me.

"Good, yes, Mexico?"

"*Sí.*" I grinned at him and got it back, like a secret between us.

Bashir came striding over. He looked down at us, hands on hips, and shook his head.

I got up and walked back over to the crowd of technicians and other extras. Bashir came after me.

"Where do you want me?" I asked.

"For now, just wait."

I mingled with the crowd. There was a squad or two of border policemen, watching with everybody else. I remembered that Bashir had once been a border policeman. He works for everybody, Riad had said. The sheikh was in the center of a cluster of his elders, trying to look like the real Moses. Everybody was staring down the slope of the hill. I walked to the edge to see what they were staring at. The slope wasn't steep and didn't drop very far until it flattened into a smooth blister of rock, a roughly circular center for the whorls of the country. The blister was bordered on the left by low brown hills and rimmed on the other side by more jagged formations that looked like sand castles brushed by waves, their tops wider than their bases. There were a few date palms in front of them, their fronds covered with yellow dust and hanging limply, like the legs of impaled spiders. I hadn't seen them before. They must have been brought in for the scene, just like we were. Palm trees trying to look like palm trees. Whores for Moses.

Two lines of men were facing each other just below us in the center of the smooth area. One group wore short purple skirts, leather breastplates, and conical helmets and carried swords and shields. The men in the other wore the longer gray robes that were supposed to be Israelite dress and had swords and spears. As I watched, the boys I'd been sitting with joined that line, making the two groups more or less equal. A track with a camera on it ran parallel to both groups. A short, fat man with an electronic megaphone in one hand strode in front of the camera. The director. He raised the megaphone to his lips and spoke into it. "We'll have the fighting now." His voice echoed among the rocks like the Voice of God.

The men began flailing at one another happily. The people around me roared as if it were a real fight. The director yelled at them to stop. Bashir repeated the cry in Arabic.

The actor playing Joshua came out and stood between the lines of Israelites and Amalekites. A technician held up a stick, and the actor hacked at it with his sword, pretending to be in a fierce fight while the camera got close-up shots of him. "Cut," the director said. The actor stopped hacking and immediately looked bored, perhaps his way of resting his face. Bashir waved up at us. Out of the corner of my eye, I saw the sheikh wave back.

A section of the low line of hills to our left swelled noiselessly and erupted into four camels and their riders. I caught my breath. The Bedouin and their animals rode out of a shimmer of heat, out of some memory inside me that had never really happened. Out of an idea of themselves. Each one had a long spear. They charged straight at the Israelites, riding through them, one leaning over the side of his camel at full gallop and lightly, contemptuously, touching Joshua on the chest with his spear point.

The Bedouin whirled back, halted, and dismounted, the way they ignored the stares and snickers of the Jericho students part of their grace. I saw the redhead walk over to one of the camels. He seemed almost to be following a script. Watching him, I felt the same helpless anger that made me scream at the characters on movie screens when I was a child, not believing they could be so stupid. Don't go down to the basement. Don't separate. That same sense of inevitability. The redhead looked up at the camel. It looked back at him out of the bottoms of its eyes and then vomited out its cud, a swollen, pink organ netted with beads and trails of slime. "A disgusting animal," the redhead said, loudly enough for us to hear, his voice echoing. The Bedu who owned the camel was walking swiftly back to it.

The boy reached up and seized the camel's nostrils. He swung the animal around and smiled up at the crowd, smiling directly at me, his grin suddenly my brother Shahid's, and he winked, as if this was something he was doing for me, a crazy act of vengeance performed for both of us against a parody. In a motion as seamless and lovely as the camel charge, the Bedu pulled a knife from under his robes and leapt at the boy. A movie-prop slash appeared on the boy's neck. He clutched it, then looked at his hand and shrieked. One of the other Jericho boys launched himself in a desperate leap, feet first into the small of the Bedu's back. A *beshul skull.* The kick knocked the Bedu away from the cut boy and into the camel's side. He bounced off, rolled, and came up holding the knife in front of him, then jumped at the second boy, who parried the knife with his prop spear. In an instant, the Jericho Arabs had charged into the other Bedouin, pummeling them with their fists and spear poles. The people around me, the Bedouin and other Arab extras, started to battle one another, spilling down into the blister. I was caught in the press of bodies for a minute, and then the fighting moved away from me. I saw the director scramble out of the way, yelling into his megaphone, signaling frantically at the cameraman, who began to film. The fighters were flailing at one another with prop spears and swords and bottles and rocks and chairs, a wild flurry of brown and red robes and rearing, panicking camels. As the camera panned them, they glanced up and then fought harder. Their mouths opened and closed, unconnected to the shrieking around me, as if the sound were out of sync. The battle moved up and down the blister, flowing among the rocks, lapping up their sides to my feet. Just below me, a Jericho boy was using a shield to fend off a Bedu trying to smash him with a bottle of Goldstar beer. The sound of shots cracked suddenly in the air, loud even against the screaming. I watched the border police charge in among the battling Amalekites and Children of Israel and Bedouin and Palestinians, as if time itself had been rent and all the mad forces of the region had finally been set loose.

Once, Shahid and Ezra and I had gone on a school *tiyul,* a field trip, to Eilat. On the bus we sang Hebrew folk songs and some popular American songs. This land was made for me and you, we sang, but they didn't mean me. At night we stayed in a trailer camp near the beach. Next to it was a big tent that had been erected by an army unit to serve as a discotheque. Its peak was open to the stars, which were obliterated by the flashing strobe lights that were popular in discos then. The music was very loud, and some of the girls from our class danced with the soldiers. The girls wore parts of their swimming costumes: halter tops and tight jeans, bikini bottoms and T-shirts. The soldiers wore bits and pieces of their uniforms: fatigue trousers and net shirts, fatigue shirts over bell-bottom jeans. Like strange hybrids. They danced wildly, throwing huge shadows on the canvas walls of the tent.

Some of the Negev Bedouin who did the "Arab work"— washing dishes, cleaning toilets—around the trailer camp filed in through the entrance as if drawn by the music. They lined up against one wall, a silent audience staring at the wild, half-naked dancers. I flushed with shame, sure that my classmates, that Ezra, were putting me into that line, connecting me to that train of bowed men, their filthy ankles showing between the hems of their ragged robes and their scuffed, oversized, ridiculous shoes; these tattered, gape-mouthed Araboush that had lined up next to Shahid and me like hidden parts of ourselves driven out by the flashes of the strobe. Their eyes gleamed with lust. Some of the dancers danced harder, the girls, I was certain, smiling mocking little smiles at me, thrusting their pelvises forward, jiggling their breasts, making their movements vulgar and obscene. After a little while the line of men sighed in unison, turned without a word, and shuffled out.

Later that night, I heard a long wavering moan coming from the desert past the border of the camp. We were sitting in front of the office shack. A naked electric light bulb burned above us, making cold shadows in the depressions in the sand. Shahid looked at me, his eyes gleaming, reflecting the light.

"It's the Bedouin," he explained to Ezra. "Let's go see."

"Not me," Ezra said, looking at the darkness beyond the camp.

We walked into the darkness, my brother and I, following the sound. The night was cold and the chanting seemed distant. The sea was next to us, reflecting a faint, silvery glow so that my hands flashed, making ghostly streaks in the corners of my eyes as I walked. There was nothing but the whispering of the sea and the sound of the chanting and I felt weightless and substanceless in the dark, a prismed reflection on the side of a bubble.

We saw the fire first, and then the tents huddled around it, thickened pieces of darkness. There was a line of men next to the fire, moving sinuously in rhythm with the chant. Some of them were still wearing the scuffed shoes they'd worn into the discotheque tent, but most of them danced barefoot, their bodies slim and straight as swords. The chanting seemed to form something sentient, a living entity of sound that had taken their bodies as its instrument. They were dancing in one place, as if their bodies were moving through time instead of space and the night was desert they had to cross. They saw us and stopped abruptly, like a line of people edging past one another for the bus, suddenly graceless. The Bedouin who'd been sitting and watching began tugging at their sleeves, whispering to them. They smiled fawningly at us: they thought us Jews from the campsite. The line of men advanced on us and they started dancing again, their movements broken and awkward, a shuffling parody of the secret dance we'd glimpsed before, their chant turned into a cloying whine. They smiled and one man stuck out his palm. Shahid cursed and shoved some money into it, and I turned and ran, back toward the lights of the camp, back to Ezra.

. . . . EZRA

In the rain and the fog, the Russian Compound looked like a drowned city just emerging from the depths. Aharon wasn't in his office, but a policeman who knew me directed me to a tin-roofed shed behind the prison building.

A small lorry was in the center of the stained concrete apron, stage-lit by a semicircle of spotlights. A group of men in coveralls hovered around it like surgeons, joking to each other with the morbid humor of doctors working on a mortally ill patient. The laughter stopped when I walked in, as if I were the patient's relative. Aharon jumped down from the rear of the lorry. Short and burly, wearing orange coveralls, he was a compacted version of my father with all of Amos's spaced-out, otherworldly dreaminess squeezed out.

"Get out of here," he said to the others, and they went, whispering in a subdued, resentful murmur. It was typical of him to kick them out rather than simply taking me to his office. My uncle's police rank isn't that high, the equivalent perhaps of an army colonel. But his job seems attached to a gossamer net of favors and debts, a complexity and depth of *protekzia,* connections, that always surprised me, even though I'd grown up a politician's son. When my father died, I had been in Germany; I would have never gotten back in time for the funeral if not for Aharon: he'd arranged a seat for me on a fully booked El Al flight, and even had the plane held at the airport until I'd arrived. When I'd thanked him, at the cemetery, he'd just nodded and said, "You owe people for that, Ezra."

"Come here," my uncle said. "Come closer."

When I did, he reached out suddenly and embraced me awkwardly, a rough imitation of a gesture he thought my father would make.

"I got your message," I said. "What did you want?"

Aharon turned from me and pulled down the rear gate of the lorry. I saw bags of grain, stacked aluminum irrigation pipes, a row of milk canisters.

"What the hell have you been doing? I get reports that you've been hanging about the Gallery, with all the other caricatures tacked onto the walls. And what's this nonsense of working for Bashir Tawfik? I've warned you about him—we know he moves drugs over the border. Breira isn't going to have anything to do with heroes whose feet are made of hashish. What are you doing, Ezra? You haven't made contact in over two weeks."

Sometime over the months since the funeral, Aharon's language about my visits to him had shifted, closing around me like a trap. I no longer dropped in—I made contact.

"I know it hasn't been easy for you," Aharon said.

"Oh, it's been easy enough. Deddy's been my friend for years."

"And what you're doing, objectively, is helping your friend, helping him by protecting him from his own naïveté."

"Objectively, I don't see any value in what I've given you. There's nothing Breira says in its private meetings that it doesn't say in public."

"What's important is the gathering of information. Dossiers. Profiles. Knowledge that's there if we need it. A man who's there if we need him."

What was important to Aharon was my participation. We both understood that. In the beginning, I hadn't been unattracted to the idea: his vocation wasn't, after all, so different from my own: it too saw the world as clean lined and sharply defined, as orderly as an architectural drawing. And in place of my own vocation was only a void anyway: my studies only a kind of cover, an attempt made out of inertia to hang on to a definition of myself that no longer fit. Even before Europe I was no longer the bright young hope, winner of awards and scholarships, that I'd been after my first war. Somewhere in the cracks between the wars I'd lost my faith in architecture, lost faith in the ability of stone and glass and metal to protect flesh. The real world took place in temporary structures jury-rigged behind prisons.

Aharon sighed, as if hooked into my thoughts. "There's something I need to show you," he said.

He climbed back into the lorry, then lifted one of the milk canisters to the edge. I took it by the bottom and the handle and brought it down. Aharon climbed off and wiped his hands on the leg of his coveralls.

He squatted down next to the canister and pried off the lid. Very carefully, he put his hand inside and pulled out a cloth-wrapped tube. He laid it gently on the floor and unrolled it. A cluster of thin aluminum wires.

"Do you recognize these?"

"Detonators."

"Yes."

"They look primitive."

He nodded, his eyes fixed to them. "You're the expert—how would you say these work?"

I touched the detonators lightly. They reminded me of something, and then I remembered what.

"Sulfuric acid inside. It drips at a controlled rate into fulminate, two chemicals run together. The canisters will be packed with TNT."

"Exactly. And you're familiar with where this type of explosive was used?"

"The King David."

"Like a reconstruction from a history book. TNT, a lorry, milk canisters. But British security wasn't as good as ours—the driver of this truck was killed when he tried to run a roadblock."

He rolled the tubes back up in the cloth.

"What am I to gather from all this, Aharon?"

"They've been using different tactics each week," he said. "Grenades under bus seats. Crates in the market. Katuyshas fired from East Jerusalem into the Jewish side of the city. But the particular choice of explosives here bothers me. They have much more modern devices and material available. This is a deliberate parallel—a statement. It's a false parallel and a false statement, but it bothers me. It speaks of an opponent who knows our history and has taken its lessons to heart."

"What's this to do with Breira?"

"Breira ignores history. Your friend Gur ignores history."

"I'm still not sure why you're telling me this."

"Because, like Breira, you're beginning to suffer the disease of doubt." He broke his squat and stood up. "Come with me. There's one more thing I need to show you. One more history lesson."

I followed him to a door at the back of the shed. We walked into another room.

The naked boy on the table was shrunken by death, his body centered on his blue, shriveled scrotum and sex, as if all his flesh had tightened to them in a last, protective convulsion.

"The driver," Aharon explained.

He went over to the garments folded neatly at the foot of the table. From one of the pockets, he pulled a folded piece of paper. He handed it to me. There was a poem on it.

I kiss the two of you, my darling
my Kalashnikov and you.

"We used to write terrible poetry like that also," Aharon said. "This could well have been a note I'd written when I was this boy's age. Even the language is the same—you notice that it's written in Hebrew, not Arabic. In fact this boy spoke Hebrew like a sabra. He *was* a sabra—an Abu Ghosh boy. Up to now the Arabs we've arrested for terrorism have been either infiltrators from across the border or from the territories. This is the first case we've had of an Israeli-Arab being directly involved in an operation. That's of great concern to me, Ezra. Our Arabs know us. Know our language. Our vulnerabilities. Know, in short, our history. They can move among us." He tapped the chest of the corpse sharply. "This boy was an Israeli-Arab, Ezra. Just like Maryam Halim."

I nodded without surprise: since I'd met Maryam in the Gallery this morning, since in fact Bashir had arranged our first meeting, I'd assumed Aharon knew—I'd assumed it was why he'd called me here.

"What are you saying?" I asked.

"Ezra, we have a dossier on her. She may have connections to the PLO."

"What do you mean by connections?"

"She's been known to make sympathetic noises about them."

"For God's sake, Aharon, what Palestinian doesn't?"

He grimaced. "Perhaps you are too close to your cover: you sound like Deddy Gur. Maryam Halim can't be regarded as just another Arab in any case—not with the father she had, not with her family name, not with the Israeli citizenship she still maintains. I thought I'd made myself clear."

"Make yourself a little clearer. Are you telling me to stay away from her or to cultivate her?"

My uncle turned from me and stared into the face of the dead boy on the table. It was smoothed blank, a tabula rasa. He traced the skin of the forehead with the nail of his thumb, drawing it down gently in a line that bisected forehead, nose, lips: splitting the face for its secrets.

"You still owe people," he said to the corpse.

The Nahlaot district is a place of narrow streets and alleys, of squeezed-together stone houses, their wooden doors painted blue or green against the evil eye, the iron railings of their balconies bleeding streaks of rust into stone. Through the crack of an open door I saw an old, shawled woman sitting on the edge of a sagging bed, three paraffin heaters arranged in front of her like attentive children, like shrines to absent children. I tried to freeze the picture in my mind. Her house around her was her flesh and memories, and for an instant I felt, like the phantom ache of a lost limb, the desire to know how to shape stone so that it could grow living into a life.

The house Breira was renting was at the bottom of the hill, near Ramban and the park. It was a squat, one-story stone house with a red tile roof and long, narrow, arched windows protected by bars and rustproofed metal shutters. Nineteenth-century Jerusalem, built when the first houses were being built outside the city walls and each house was a walled city itself. Built for sieges.

The door was open; I walked inside.

Most of the interior was taken by a large central room furnished with frayed Old City rugs and cushions and straw mats. There was an ancient, broken-backed horsehair sofa, its surface shined thin with use, in the center of the room, but the dozen or so people there were sitting on the floor. Some of them had blankets draped over their shoulders against the cold. It made the room seem like the meeting place of a coven or cabal. A picture of Breira in the minds of its enemies. A suddenly clear phrase drifted to me from the murmur of conversation; it formed like a labeling caption under the people there: "But they're heroes in the Arab world." I felt a rise of contempt. Sometimes I felt that my uncle was right, that I was among my enemies when I came to Breira.

A boy with a dough white face smiled up at me. "Ezra? It's been a long time." He waved around. "How do you like our new palace?"

"What happened to the old one?"

"Too many cockroaches. Too many cockroaches and bomb threats." He jerked his thumb toward the back. "Deddy's in there."

I walked through the room to a small bedroom in the back. Deddy was sitting with Yael Ziegler, their backs against the wall, their legs outstretched on the rumpled bed. As soon as she saw me, Yael put her hand on Deddy's shoulder in a quick, defiant signal of allegiance. On the night she learned of her brother's death in the Sinai, I slept with her, a misguided gesture of comfort neither one of us has forgiven me for. Deddy put the papers he was holding in his right hand under the wing of his stump and raised his foot at me in greeting. An old joke between us.

During the last war our reserve unit held a position, a sandbag fortress we'd retaken after it had been overrun, against the Syrians for three days, helping to buy time for the rest of the army to finish mobilizing against the inefficient Arabs, who could never mount a surprise attack against us and who of course had done just that. Deddy and I managed to somehow live through those three days, a trick not accomplished by anyone else in our unit. After the war, we endured several embarrassing weeks seeing our pictures—the two of us covered with blood and slime being pulled like newborns from a trench—on the pages of every Israeli newspaper. But our "heroism" was simply that we survived—we spent most of those three days hiding like rats in the bowels of that sandbag fortress, befouling ourselves and crying like babies. I can't remember the exact moment near the end when Deddy was hit by Katuysha shrapnel, receiving the wound that would cost him his left arm. Sometimes I think of the limb as being slowly pounded off in the course of those three days.

When I first saw Deddy again, in the hospital, I walked right past his room: I couldn't imagine the bald old man who I glimpsed through the door—his face mashed and swollen, his nose propped by tubes—to be Deddy. Not until I checked the room number again and forced myself to admit it. Deddy's remaining arm and one leg had been broken and were supported by straps; when I came in he looked down at his helpless body, his eyes fluttering in panic. Then a beatific smile came over his face, and he offered me his left leg to shake, as if not knowing what limb to hand me had been the cause of his concern. I laughed with relief at the joke, at Deddy's self-mockery, his concern to demonstrate his basic intactness, the survival of his Deddy-ness to me. I laughed until the tears came, Deddy joining in, until a nurse hushed us up. She looked at the two of us and called a doctor, who sedated Deddy and tried to have me admitted.

Deddy looked at me thoughtfully. It was the same long, assessing look Bashir had given me, checking my sobriety: a look I was getting used to from my friends. Deddy massaged the end of his stump. A slight wince of pain crossed his face, and I remembered, my recollections reminding me, that he was supposed to go back to the hospital last week.

"Weren't you due for your checkup?"

He shrugged. "Sure. But I don't know what they're checking, every year. It's not going to *regenerate,* I tell them."

He smiled, the deeply engraved scar lines that widened his mouth turning it into a sardonic rictus.

"Listen," he said, "did I tell you how Dayan came to the hospital, when I was there? He comes into the ward and he asks the man in the first bed, a man with one leg, how he's doing. Couldn't be better, the guy says, the treatment is wonderful. So Dayan goes to the second bed, where there's a man with no arms, and asks the same question. Uncle, I'm going to rehabilitate with grace and courage and take a productive place in society, the man says. And you? Dayan asks, touched, weeping out of his one eye. He's talking to a guy now whose entire body has been amputated—he's nothing but a head centered on a fluffy pillow. Not too good, the head says. Everyone is shocked. Who is this ingrate, this prima donna? Thing is, general, the head says, I had to wait five hours in line this morning to see the dentist."

Deddy brayed delightedly at his own joke.

"I hate it when he's gutsy," Yael said. She looked at me curiously. "What brings you around, Ezra? We haven't seen you in weeks."

"We're lucky," Deddy said. "The last time Ezra dropped

out of my life I didn't see him for two years. We usually only get together for wars or funerals—whenever he loses a father or I lose a limb. I'm relieved it's not either occasion this time."

"Deddy," Yael said.

Deddy grinned his clown's grin at me.

"I met an old friend," I said. "Maryam Halim."

"Really?" Deddy nodded. "I remember the Halims. I thought they'd moved to the West Bank."

"Arabs?" Yael said, like a curse. She ran her fingers through the blond, tousled nest of her hair, her eyes bruised by the shadows of the room. She and her brother had been close, as close as twins, as if they still shared the same veins: she was in Breira because she hated the war almost as much as she hated the people who'd killed him.

"Maryam's at the university now," I said. "She wanted to come to a Breira meeting."

Yael looked at me thoughtfully. "And after all this time you ran right over to arrange it. How about you, Ezra? Do you plan to come more often now, come to a few Breira meetings with your old Arab friend?"

"Whatever it takes to bring him back in the fold," Deddy said smoothly. "Where has she been, Ezra—at Bir Zeit?" He named the Palestinian college near Ramallah.

"No, in the States."

"Ah."

I looked at Deddy, feeling a sharp tug of doubt at bringing Maryam to his attention: he had something in mind for her already.

Yael clicked her tongue against the roof of her mouth. "We don't need Arabs."

Deddy reached over and gently erased the words from her lips with his thumb.

"It's important to show that we're not just talking to ourselves. Not just masturbating."

"Look, she just wanted to meet you, talk," I said.

Deddy looked at me innocently. "Yes?"

"Don't get her too involved."

"What's worrying you, *boychik?*"

"How far do you want her to bend over, Deddy? To save you from masturbating?"

Deddy blinked, as if considering the image.

"Only a little," he said.

There were dabs of shit on both doorposts of the apartment when I got home: the one on the right was placed where a mezuzzah would be, if I had one. The warnings, signs of contempt, whatever shit represented to whoever was doing this, had increased over the last months, since my "involvement" with Breira. My apartment wasn't the only one in the building struck. Dr. Birnbaum, a pathologist at Hadassah Hospital who lived on the floor above, had had his door smeared with fecal swastikas, drawn presumably by some ultraorthodox opponents of autopsies. The swastikas must have brought back memories to Birnbaum, who came to Palestine from Germany after Kristallnacht.

I went into the kitchen, pushed the dirty dishes aside, and ran water over a rag. A pan stood on a burner, the burnt, rubbery egg congealed to its center staring back at me. I took a dry rag from the rack under the sink, wet another one, then went outside and cleaned the door. I threw the rags into the garbage cans in front of the building, went back to the kitchen, and washed the dishes in the sink, dried and stacked them, and scoured the pan. Then I spent an hour cleaning the apartment: vacuuming, dusting, putting everything in its place, as if my father were watching me. The apartment was my inheritance. He'd left it to me along with enough savings and insurance money for me to be a full-time student for a year, along with his propensity to cultivate the doubts of the soul.

I got a bottle of beer from the refrigerator, then sat down at the kitchen table and thumbed through my textbooks, some drawings I'd been trying to do, and my notes. The drawings were unfinished and my notes were fragmentary. When I'd decided to make my last attempt at getting my degree, I'd had, I think, an appealing vision of myself sealed in the haven of the apartment and its walls of books. But the incestuous huddle of Jerusalem cafés was more beckoning: in the Gallery I'd found that a drunken self-disgust was the coin of entry, everyone was glad to see me, and in the pleasant glow of a few too many cognacs every conversation sparkled with brilliance.

I finished the beer and took another and tried to make sense out of my notes. They were for a city planning course I'd enrolled in; I worked, one year, for the Jerusalem Planning Commission. My chosen project was no less than a plan for Jerusalem, though I hadn't gotten past the preliminary analysis. Jerusalem is built on a series of ridges; its aesthetics, that is, its impact on the eye as a unique city (I'd written), its very quality of being Jerusalem in fact, can be shown to hinge on an imaginary walker's ability to see the city's coherence with its surrounding hills and valleys, i.e., there are certain identified key points on the ridge lines of the city where one can see and sense this weave. If you imagine the city and its hills as a tapestry, these key points can be likened to openings through which you'd thread your sight to weave the composite together. It becomes clear, therefore (my notes asserted), that these points of visual weaving (my phrase) needed to remain open, that is, not blocked from view by tall buildings, and that further, the best way to achieve this effect was both by limiting the heights of buildings and by turning the identified view sites (IVS's?) into areas where no building construction was allowed, e.g., public parks. What I'd found in fact was that many of these key visual points (the phrase sounded less awkward) had been identified by the municipality, which had deliberately turned them into garbage dumps: a park couldn't be sold to a developer, but a dump could. Some of the sites had in fact already been sold—for handsome sums paid in foreign currency—by the city, and high-rise buildings—hotels and condominium apartment ventures—had been built upon them; in addition, the developers, mostly American, swelled the city coffers with fines for violating building height codes (where the limit in Jerusalem was seven stories, they'd built twenty-five), which they simply figured as part of their operating expenses. Each building erected blocked a key visual point and hence the cohesive quality that made Jerusalem Jerusalem for everyone except those (mostly foreigners "investing in the Holy City") who could afford the view: thus the municipality, chuckling at its shrewdness, sold its birthright for a few American dollars.

The beer was gone and I hadn't solved anything yet, so I went to the cupboard and pulled out a bottle of Stock cognac. I poured myself a glass, still looking at the jumble of my notes, at my own general lack of cohesiveness. Of course it wasn't as simple as I was making it out either: the money the municipality earned at the expense of aesthetics went to low-income housing, much needed—the pragmatic always needed to outweigh the ideal. And of course there were political considerations, considerations of realpolitik that couldn't be ignored by architects and planners: neighborhoods needed to be built to consolidate borders, buildings designed to deliberately dwarf, break, ring, i.e., my chosen profession tried, as a spoiled child does, to smash the world into the shape of its own convenient, private vision.

The phone rang, jangling the private vision I was trying not to think about. It was Deddy, the living doubts of my soul come calling. He'd made arrangements for a "seminar" tomorrow at the American School. He'd already called Maryam Halim. She wanted to come. Look, it was her idea. Did I still have those extra boxes of pamphlets? Good. Bring them. Did I understand that he'd only left them as an excuse to ensure my participation? Like an article of clothing left at a lover's apartment? Not that he had any designs on me, beyond political, thank you. Would I be there? Good. Be early. Be well. Don't worry. Good-bye.

I hung up. The bottle of cognac stood next to my books like an easy choice. I poured another glass, went into the living room, and turned on the television. There still hadn't been any arrests for the car bombing. Last night, again near Zion Square, a taxi driver had been found murdered, strangled and stuffed into the trunk of his car, his body booby-trapped with charges attached to a powerful bomb placed in a milk canister—it had been disarmed by a sapper. In Ramat Gan, the police chief had been stabbed during a riot that took place after a soccer game with the Jerusalem team. I turned off the television.

I got up and filled my glass again, then went back and sat in front of the silent set. In my father's chair. A picture of him sitting in it formed in my mind. His face, pale-lit by the screen, had suddenly looked to me to be the face of an old man, its skin parchment thin and finely veined. I'd felt

an ice-cold shock. Until then I'd regarded Amos's protesta-
tions of old age as a form of nagging. His hands, dangling
over the armrests, had still looked big to me, the veins in
them corded—in his youth they'd shaped a nude brown hill
into a village, built dreams into walls; in the Knesset they'd
clutched passionately, pulling ringing phrases from the air as
plants from dry soil—but they were the only part of him
that had survived intact. I'd just been demobilized and had
decided to travel in Europe, then take the scholarship I'd
been awarded in Germany, but seeing for the first time the
death stamped into his flesh, I'd almost changed my mind. I
wished I had.

I took a long drink, letting it burn down my throat, filling hollows. The blank television screen formed a point of
focus, a key visual point I needed to keep open, step back
from and see the whole picture. I pressed my knuckles into
my eyes, making patterns of light, then pain. When I took
my hands away, the patterns stayed on the screen in a
spreading stain that gathered the images I'd been resisting,
the broken film that ran nightly in my mind. The lights came
on and there they were, the same cast, the same extras, as if
they were just moved from village to village. The people
pushing against the barricades with their hatred exuding
from them like an intensification of their sweat and stink, an
oozing from some new gland they'd developed in reaction
to us. With the same boy of fourteen or fifteen, head shaved
for lice, scalp shaled with dirt, screaming in my face and
grabbing the barricade rail and shaking it in rhythm with his
screams. With the same woman standing next to him, his
mother or aunt or even his wife for all I knew about him,
her own screams coaxing his, coiling tighter and tighter in
my stomach, and her mouth working and the spittle splat-
tering my visor and the same rock sailing out of the crowd

and hitting against Dov's helmet and Baruch growling at me to hurry the fuck up. Shit, sergeant architect, Deddy would say to me, the same dialogue each time, our own script for the crack between the wars. Absolutely, captain policeman, I'd reply, and turn and walk away, raising my faceplate, the woman's spit hanging from it. The air suddenly very still and hot on my face and silence and the thistles around the house standing hollow, stiff, and brittle in the heat of the day and making myself look up from them at the house, put together without coherence, a jumble of stones whose pattern eludes me, shaped according to the needs of a life I wasn't inside—the architecture of an alien mind. So I check the wires again and look around to make sure everyone is clear again and I get behind the low stone wall and peer over the top, the wire running from my hand to the house and images and echoes of the generations of the house: children and mothers and fathers and grandmothers and great-grandfathers, fluttering in pulses of current through the wire, passing into me, an accumulation of small weights. And I'm called back to do it again, the film running backward, me a comic figure with jerky, speeded-up movements. Do it, sergeant architect, Deddy whispers, do it and we can all go home, so I do it so we can all go home, push the button and there is a series of brief, barking explosions and the thistles sway and break and the main section of the house swells in one last and greater instant of solidity and then the walls collapse inward, the lessons of the classroom meeting the lessons of the world. Beauty, Deddy says, the Brenner trademark, no big bang, no dramatics, not another house touched. With only the yellow dust hanging in the heated air and thinning and drifting and some of it settling on my face, into my skin, and cracks spreading through the foundations.

. . . . MARYAM

My father liked to take my brother and me to the small
section of the Israel Museum that held imprisoned relics of
the Arab past of Jerusalem. He enjoyed lapping up second
chances from the fresh wells of our vision, he said. "Today,"
he'd say, "the Umayyad caliphs," and Shahid would roll his
eyes at me and off we'd go.

"Why, Daddy?" I asked, after another lesson about Abd
al-Malik or Arabic calligraphy.

"I'm giving you weapons."

When I was thirteen years old, in the Israel Museum, one
of his weapons pierced me and I bled. Resting, sitting on a
bench, I felt the liquid warmth between my legs and looked
down in horror at the stain on the front of the thin cotton
dress I wore.

"Daddy," I said, my voice breaking, and his eyes brushed
the front of my dress and fled away. "You see, the Abbasids
really had no interest in Jerusalem," he said.

"Daddy," I said, starting to cry, and his face clouded

with anger. Shahid looked down at me and then at him and swore.

"What the hell's the matter with you?"

"Don't speak to me like that."

Shahid swore again and walked away. My father turned from me, his body stiff. I clutched at myself, crying, people staring, my father's eyes fixed to the display case. Then I saw Shahid coming back, tugging at the arm of a large Jewish woman. Her eyes were bright with concern.

"Come along, sweetheart, it's nothing," the woman said, and led me out of Arab Jerusalem, to the ladies' room.

When I came out, Shahid kissed me on the forehead and said not to worry; he'd take care of me. He put his arm around my shoulders and we began walking to the exit.

"Where's Daddy?" I asked.

"They're stuffing him. They have a special exhibit room for assholes," Shahid said. And we exited laughing, my brother and I.

And a few years later, when it was his turn to bleed, there was nothing, absolutely nothing, I could do about it.

And what I want to ask is this: what weapons could our father give us, when he refused to see us bleed?

. . . . DEDDY

So, Ezra, *boychik,* why am I trying so hard? Maybe because I'm simply tired. Like now. Another endless meeting and I step out of the buzz of voices into the air, my bird-wing stump hurting like hell, rubbed raw by all that clever, caustic dialogue, and the mask that's been eating my face hurting like hell too. So I need a friend who knows I'm not the mask. That simple. Who remembers my face as he remembers me whole, when this stump had an appendage attached that I could use to scratch myself and pick my nose at the same time—the height of convenience. I need you at these meetings, buddy. Like that time we went to the Buddhist ceremony in Ramat Gan—your father arranged it with the Burmese ambassador, remember?—and we sat cross-legged and shoeless in the little house in which they had the service: meditation, chanting, incense burning, and while it was still going on we snuck away, down into the basement of the house so that we could discuss what we'd seen in excited whispers—the two Jews in the basement with their need to put everything into words while it was still going on silently above their heads. (Your father was into his intercultural trip then, remember? That "progressive" weirdo gymnasia he had you attend for two years, with the kids of six rich Jewish-Persian families, three Asian embassies, fifteen old leftist-Zionist families—and of course, the Halims.) Only these Breira meetings, *boychik*—they're all in the basement. Endless analysis, belly-button contemplation. All those words buzzing around me. Gur, it's useless, why have a rally there? Those people, foreigners; they're not part of the situation. They're dilettantes, students here for a year; their asses aren't on the line. I say, listen, I'm tired of hearing where their asses are. Does an ass on a line or even sticking out from a line weight it with the heavy, doughlike cheeks of moral legitimacy? What's the determining factor? How far it sticks out, this ass? If you can wipe it with bullets? Tell me, ladies and gentlement, *rabotai,* how much moral legitimacy does the loss of one limb give me? Would I be more moral if I lost four limbs? Would that make me more of a mensch? Like the guy on the pillow with dental problems. Or the guy in our ward, no joke, *boychik,* who wanted a handle sewn on his morally legitimate ass so he could be rehabilitated as a suitcase. Their asses, I say eloquently, the buttocks of these students, these Portnoys and Woody Allens, these, in two words, American Jews, yes, they are in the debate. Some have come here to, after all, find themselves—they want to be Hebrew peasants and warriors after bouts with Buddhism, wrestlings with the *I Ching.* So what do you say, let's sneak something inside them to find. Otherwise they'll go to the settlements and find themselves kicking some Arab asses out of their homes. Or they'll go home and be blank checks, and the government will take over sixty thousand more dunams of Arab lands and announce it's to protect their security on Long Island. So it's important, I said. I said until I was tired of my words, of the mask eating my face. Politics. Bolitics, as the Arabs say. Not a false face, all the worse. A mask I put on voluntarily. That I can't take off, *boychik*. Even as it consumes me. How, you ask, can a mask eat a face? First a nose, then eyebrows, then eyes, then the lips . . .

So, I needed you. Friend Ezra, who knew me when I had my ass and all my limbs and no mask. Once upon a time, I didn't say to my comrades, once upon a time I had a friend, I was blown to atoms with him, we came back mixed. In one explosion I lost an arm and became a human being. In many explosions he lost his hands, his fine architect's hands, blown off bit by bit. First a fingernail, then a joint . . . bones splintered, pounded off, useless. So he'll be my arm and I'll be his heart and together we'll make a whole man. And once upon a time my friend had a friend, an Arab. Listen. When we played soccer and the mob would yell at Shahid—Arab bastard, son of a whore—we'd edge away uneasily, as if from some muffled crowd roar in our own hearts, but Ezra would plant himself in front of Shahid, catching a thrown bottle with his face once and grinning, smiling that he could give a little, bleed. Bleeding and glancing at the balcony where Maryam stood, to be sure she saw. So this is in him, in my friend, buried under the debris of the houses his bleeding hands built and demolished. So once upon a time my friend had a friend, an Arab, and fuck the Americans, I've arranged this little rally so she'll be there and together we'll pull him from that muddy, debris-filled trench; we'll pull him out into the light. But I didn't say that to my comrades, *boychik*.

Look, sergeant architect, I'm passing the Monastery of the Cross now, and what would you have done with this building, with its too thick walls, its white stone faintly luminous, an ill-defined yet massive presence in the dark? But I bet you'd be able to define it, eh, sergeant architect? Those measurements you memorized, that you'd recite like a poem. Three hundred and fifty kilograms of TNT that become two hundred and fifty thousand liters of gas that heat to three thousand degrees centigrade as they expand at one hundred thousand kilometers per hour, creating an atmospheric pressure of five hundred thousand pounds per square centimeter. That'll do it. So much for that. Powdered stone, the bones and gristle of your hands glistening in it.

And who is this odd bird peering at me belligerently from the darkness? A Hasid, pasty flesh, black gabardines. (How we teased them when we were kids, huh, *boychik?* Like young Nazis or cossacks.) A fanatic of the first order, no doubt, with his pale ax blade of a face cleaving the air toward me. A skinny little creep.

"Gur!" he says.

I smile my best bolitician's smile, the mask slipping smoothly into place.

"Enemy of Israel!" He sprays my face with spittle. "Comforter of Amalek! May the Lord cut off your other arm and all the arms of our enemies, *amen sela.*"

The mask slips. I tuck in my other arm and flap both stumps at him. "The Lord made me a bird." I caw at him, at this black crow. He looks at me in astonishment, then an oily triumph spills over his face. I've been cursed by madness, *amen sela.*

"Consider the birds," I say, flapping. "They want not. Their feather asses aren't on the line. They fly over. They maintain a certain detachment."

He stares at me.

"You're not Gur," he says in disappointment.

I walk away from him, down Ramban. Just a little vacation from bolitics, *rabotai,* ladies and gentlement. But don't worry. I'm still here.

Are you still here, *boychik?* I can sit down on this rock
next to the road and close my eyes here in the dark and see
us, see a line of sunlight moving over the plateau and revealing things. Someone slowly lifting a rock and displaying
the squirming grubs under it. Smashed tanks and half-tracks,
smeared insects. The light on my fingers as if they've grown
back with its lengthening. My fingers pale against the gray
metal of the gun. The light glittering off the piles of debris
in front of our position. Behind us, the fortress, a broken
hump of piled sandbags, a crouched beast, hit in many places,
the sand pouring like blood from rents in its side. No. You,
sergeant, you're the architect, you have to see the world in
metaphors. But I'm just a wingless bird. A bird has no metaphors. A bird sees the world as it is. Thus: behind us a dirty
heap of sandbags. Before us, garbage. Piles of debris. Discarded ration cans, dead cows, their stomachs up and bellies
smooth with bloat, like rubber gloves someone had blown
up and tied off. The twisted metal of weapons and tanks and
half-tracks blown into skeletal fossils, the bodies of the boys
we'd come to relieve mixed in, their asses on the line. A
Syrian's ass high and bare, locked in an obscene thrust, the
rest of his uniform intact, his face down in a black pool of
scummy water. Israelis and Syrians still locked together, teeth
sunk into flesh. Shells thudding into the mud, raising and
rearranging the dead, the shock waves moving through the
earth to the trench, through their veins and bones and skin
to mine. You and I hugging each other and quivering like
the mud, blood leaking from our noses and mouths and ears
and our sad asses on the line, congealing us, you staring
wide-eyed as if every house you'd ever blown up was exploding in front of your face, dead houses rising with the
dead who were rising to repopulate them. And I have to
scream and hit you and the others with the butt of my

weapon, making them fire, a strength running through me from the strength of explosions, a strength I loved so much then that even while I had it I knew I'd have to spend the rest of my life fighting it, the rest of my life in a mask, or it would possess me like a drug.

And then I'm rushing out of myself and a light broke inside itself and intensified impossibly and I saw everything. The light was very clear and everything I was and you were rushed to a point and came together in brilliance at that point. And then I'm back, mashed and gushing out of myself, you and I mixed into the mud of the trench. Your eyes staring at me, rolling, your skin grained with dirt. You getting a tourniquet on me, using the barrel of an Uzi to wind it tight. A line of tanks and men moving toward us. Getting your arm around me and dragging me back, into a narrow slit in the sandbags. Clawing down the bags behind us as you go, pulling me into the blackness. Pulling me and pulling me until the tunnel widens a little and the two of us are encapsulated in the center of the collapsed fortress, the compressed heat and a sense of weight all around us in the blackness, the sandbag walls pressing us like hot flesh as if we were—yes, I see your metaphor—as if we were in some hot, foul internal cavity. Shells falling outside, their noise like angry voices heard through walls, a child overhearing his parents arguing about him. Blasts of sand stinging my face and peppering my body. The sandbags trembling, their weight around me shuddering, my open veins flowing into, staunched by sand. I feel myself being overcome by a heavy, lulling complacency, as if I'm being filled by the weight of sand. As if I'm being absorbed, digested. In the beast I had to be shit out of to become a man, *boychik*. If you want to be metaphorical.

We're mixed, sergeant architect, you schmuck. Don't you think I know what you're doing? You're so bad at it, too.

You and your late-night meetings and your mysterious
phone calls and your self-contempt.

I knew it from the funeral. What an affair, huh, *boychik?*
Everyone who was anyone was there, remember? Friends
and enemies crowded the section of the cemetery reserved
for the dead of the War of Independence—your mother,
wisely knocked off at Castel, gone ahead to reserve space for
your father. And his contemporaries and peers mixed among
the graves of the liberation war like examples of what the
fallen might have become if they'd lived and corrupted. Begin made an appearance, Shamir; Sharon was conspicuously
absent. Dayan came, Peres and Allon, Bar-Lev and Elazar.
The ones the wheel was carrying to the top and the ones the
wheel was grinding under. And then Amnon Sapir and the
old pioneers who'd founded Beit Harim with your parents.
Forming a small weathered circle themselves, as if they'd
carried the perimeter of the kibbutz with them to protect
them from the corruptions of the city. You always have a
home with us, Ezra. You shook hands. Jet-lagged, Germany-
lagged. Dazed. Thank you. Yes, you understood it was pain-
less. A quick stroke. Better not to linger. Yes, you were fine.
A bit tired. Yes, if you needed anything you'd be sure to
call. Yes, it was unfortunate that people seemed to come
together only at such times. Yes, one could say that architecture was a substantial and useful discipline. Certainly people needed places to live.

All the people there, only coming together at such a time,
as if they'd finally found a place to live. Jews and Arabs
together in the graveyard. Shayhk Nussiyeh of Nazareth, the
rabid moderate. Salah Nashishibi, the mukhtar of Ibten, the
village near your father's kibbutz. The former mayor of East
Jerusalem. Rubbing elbows in the graveyard with Naim the
greengrocer and Maurice who runs the shoe-repair stand be-

hind the Beit Hakerem supermarket. All in the graveyard where, a few years before, we'd been born, me and you, sergeant architect.

So there I am. Standing at the edge of the crowd. My invisible arm aching to embrace you. You walk over and embrace me. I'm sorry. How have you been? A stiffness between us that we both knew came from more than the distance of the two years we hadn't seen each other, more than our meeting at Amos's funeral. We'd argued bitterly before you'd left—the idea of Breira, of soldiers protesting their war, you'd said rather melodramatically, was a betrayal of the dead we left back on the Golan. But your real anger, *boychik,* admit it, was that it was the first time in our lives that we'd argued bolitics. That seemed a deeper betrayal to you. That I'd had to don the mask. That the situation had at last been poured like a foul, sticky glue over all our intricacies, into the hollow at the very center of ourselves.

So you hugged me in front of gravestones, and over your shoulder I saw your uncle, in his full police regalia, staring at me. He walked over, some ever-shortening rope taut between our eyes, and pried you away and kissed you, staring at me, and at that moment I knew how he'd use you. When we were kids, your father and your uncle fought for you like rival religions fighting for a soul. Now here he was, a squat vulture. (But it's my turn to fight for your soul, buddy.) Are you all right? he asked you. Money? You were fine, you had the apartment, Amos had had insurance. You had architecture. And he nodded and waved it all away impatiently, glaring at you and putting his hand on your shoulder, claiming you. Turning you away and the two of you walking to the grave, whispering like conspirators.

But here's Yael's apartment now, *boychik,* so I have to say good night, though I don't know why I bother. I go to her and she looks through me for you anyway, just as your uncle looked through you for me. Why do I take it? Listen, once I read about a missionary and an Eskimo hunter. The missionary was interested in Eskimo customs, and he could never understand the prayer his Eskimo friend would mutter after he'd kill a seal, then eat its raw and bloody liver. Finally, he recorded the phrase and brought the recording to a friend of his whose Inuit was better. His friend told him that what the prayer meant, what his Eskimo buddy was saying was, It's better than nothing. *Amen sela.*

Yael opens the door and stares at me silently, searching my face. *"B'seder?"* she asks, a prayer that means Is there any order in the world? I kiss her and hold her for a moment; my missing arm and hand aching, reaching invisibly and seeking substance. Encased in the flesh of her back and shoulders like something unborn.

I'd parked the Land-Rover, a wreck Deddy and I had brought back to life, on the dirt path behind my apartment building. I loaded it with the boxes of pamphlets he'd asked me to keep. The air was crisp, and a Bedu was herding a flock of goats in the boulder-strewn field between Beit Hakerem and the ridge of Bayit Vegan. I stopped and looked at them before I turned the ignition key. The goats, their breath steaming, made jumps and flows of black around the white stones, silent, they and their robed herdsman a last, lingering dream of the city before it fully awoke.

I turned the key, breaking the silence, bumped out over the path, and turned left on Herzl Boulevard. Near the military cemetery I saw two women, their heads draped in black shawls. Dawn mourners. They were standing in the area where, on the first day of the last war, my reserve outfit had mustered. We'd thought the location fittingly morbid. Deddy, our leader, his face glowing with a chance for irony, had formed us into hora circles and we'd sung and danced ironically in front of the stones.

I drove past Bayit Vegan and into Kiriat Hayovel, made a right onto the street where the college was, and parked next to the kiosk near the school entrance. I was early, but I saw Maryam's red Vespa parked at the curb. I bought some rolls from the kiosk and sat next to the bike. The American School, across from me, was a single, block-long, five-story building. It had a streaked marble facade and the slightly shabby, unkempt look I associated with yeshivas, religious institutions. There were a number of youth movement and travel posters taped around the front door, a scatter of litter below them.

Maryam came around from the side of the building and stood in front of me. "Good morning," she said, smiling. For an instant her eyes met mine and her smile broadened, encompassing our past again, as if it were a joke on the world we shared. She flapped her hand at the school. "Arabs and Jews and cakes and grapefruit juice."

I handed her a roll. She sat down next to me and ate it.

"I hope it's that peaceful," I said. "How did Deddy convince you to come?"

"He told me he needed help with his English, that he'd heard I'd gone to school in the States. His English is fine. It's the trick of giving a child responsibility to get her involved."

Deddy's old Renault pulled up behind the Land-Rover. Yael and Deddy got out. He nodded to me and greeted Maryam.

"Thank you for coming."

"Ever so much," Yael said sweetly.

Deddy ignored her. "Look, we may have a problem," he said. "The school called me—apparently they've decided our speaking here might not be a good idea. Come in with us, Maryam, help me speak to them."

She grinned at me, as if to say, You see? "Coming?" she asked.

"I'll wait here."

I watched her walk into the building, past the posters, seeing them for a startlingly vivid instant through her eyes: flowers blooming in the desert, blond, unironic hora dancers in front of the gravestones of her people.

After ten minutes, the door opened and they came back out. Deddy was smiling faintly.

"We can hold the seminar outside the building if we want," he explained. "At our own risk. They'll even let us use their tables."

"We're targets outside," Yael said.

"What use are we if we hide?"

"Look," I said to Maryam. "I'm sorry I got you involved."

"Don't be so arrogant." She smiled grimly. "It's my choice. My *breira.*"

She turned away. Deddy grinned at me. "Don't be so arrogant," he said. "Help me unload."

We unloaded the boxes from the Land-Rover and the sound equipment from his car, then set up the two tables the school gave us near the front of the building. I watched Maryam and Yael stacking pamphlets about Jewish-Arab cooperation on the tables, as if they were building a wall between themselves.

Deddy flicked his finger against the mike. "We're going to get killed out here," he said.

Two more cars pulled up. Breira people piled out and immediately began arguing about the location. A small crowd of students had gathered at the entrance of the college. Deddy talked to them as he ran the wires from the mike and speakers into the building. A tall, long-haired boy in an Old City sheepskin jacket nodded vigorously at Deddy's words, while two girls wearing the same sort of jacket shook their heads vehemently. It was like watching a pantomime of polarization. People were sticking their heads out of the windows of the apartment building across the street. Passersby began clustering at the pamphlet tables and arguing with Breira members. Deddy's instant bazaar. His genius for dancing in front of the stones. I felt suddenly as I had when I'd gone to Bashir's movie: I didn't know what the hell I was doing here. A man in a sleeveless undershirt leaned out of one of the apartment windows, cupped his hands and yelled something unintelligible, then disappeared inside.

Deddy stepped behind the mike. There was an electronic feedback whine and the crowd grew quiet. He began speaking in English, addressing the American students. *"Debair Ivrit!"* someone shouted. "Speak Hebrew!" A mutter of approval ran through the Israeli portion of the crowd. Someone yelled a curse. It set off an answering ripple of nervous giggles. A blond man, his face creased with rage, cupped his hands and shouted, "Gur! What about the taxi driver who was strangled yesterday? Do you want us to talk to murderers?" He stared directly at me, his eyes burning. "Who else?" I heard Deddy say. There were catcalls from the crowd. Deddy raised his stump, brandishing it like moral authority. What was happening here was our problem, not our fate, he said, as if he were speaking only to me. But I believed that houses should be built that belonged to their landscape; that is to say, I believed in the utter power of the murderous ground I lived on to shape its inhabitants. In the name of something no more or less holy than living space, two peoples were trying to erase each other; in the process, each was erasing itself, Deddy said. You still owe people, Aharon had said. "Speak Hebrew!" someone yelled. But I wasn't sure if words still meant the same thing to me as they did to Aharon.

I looked over at Maryam, standing behind the table near Deddy. A large, big-bellied man with a small, thin woman hanging on to his arm like an extra appendage, walked up to the front of the table. The man was drinking from a bottle of Coke. He put it down on the table, yawned elaborately, and looked around with sleepy surprise at the milling people. He might as well have worn a sign.

I moved toward him, through the crowd. When I was near, the small woman suddenly stepped in front of me. She winked, as if we were accomplices. "We can't let them turn us into murderers too," I heard Deddy say.

"What shit," the fat man said to me, as if we were sharing a secret joke.

He picked the bottle up and turned it upside down, spilling the Coke over the pamphlets. Maryam was staring at him as if she remembered him from someplace. "Leave me alone," she said.

The man smiled at her. *"Kus emuk,"* he said, in Arabic. Your mother's cunt.

"Shut up," I said.

The man turned his smile to me. "Not only a cunt, but a real Arab cunt," he said confidentially.

He reached over and prodded her breasts with the bottom of the Coke bottle. Once, twice. I hit his wrist with the edge of my hand. The bottle dropped and shattered. The man lunged at me, grabbing a handful of my shirt. I snapped my arm straight out, the heel of my hand going sharply into the bridge of his nose. A look of astonishment, blood, snot, blossomed in the center of his face. I hit into it with my fist, dropping my shoulder and getting my weight into it. Then I hit him again, Aharon's man, punctuating my resignation from history. Then my arms were being held and Deddy was next to me and the man was heaped at my feet.

Deddy put a foot on his shoulder and pushed him over. He flopped onto his side and began vomiting in small heaves. Deddy squatted down and patted his back. "Good, you son of a whore," he muttered, so that only I would hear. I had no memory of how he'd gotten there.

The whole world had stopped and was staring at me, Maryam in its front row.

"I don't understand you," Deddy muttered to me, standing up. "You know better, Ezra. You know it was a provocation."

"I was provoked."

He shook his head in disgust. Yael stared at me, and then, deliberately, at Maryam. "And you don't understand him," she said to Deddy. She walked away.

Deddy wouldn't look at me. "You'd better get out of here," he said. "It will calm things down."

I looked around, focusing. Someone was shouting; a man was shaking his fist in my direction. Three Breira people surrounded him and began talking soothingly. I saw Yael move smoothly in front of a stocky man in a red jogging suit who was gesticulating angrily. She began talking to him earnestly, touching her chest, putting his anger into herself. The microphone had been knocked over, and then I had a delayed memory of Deddy leaping from it when the fight started, coming to me as he'd once come to me running down the length of a trench.

The small woman had knelt by the man I'd beaten and was cradling his head.

"Maybe we'd better call an ambulance," I said.

She spat at me. "Leave us alone, you cocksucker," she said, in hard, Brooklyn-accented English.

Maryam tugged my arm.

"Let's go," she said. "I think the seminar is over."

·.·

I followed her Vespa, Maryam's hair flying out after her like the flag of my folly. She wove through the traffic to the Old City, to the parking lot across from Jaffa Gate. I pulled in next to her.

"Are you all right?" Maryam asked.

"I just feel foolish."

She was staring at me as if she'd never seen me before. "Let's get something to eat," she said finally. "I have a vile taste in my mouth."

A light rain had started to fall while we were driving, and the stones in the city wall were faintly luminous, jewel prismed under a skin of wetness. We walked into the Old City. The aged smell was very strong in the rain. We went down into the narrow streets of the souk. Racks of long, black Arab dresses, their fronts splashed with bright red and yellow dabs of embroidery, hung on both sides, high up on the pressing walls. Underneath them old women wearing the same dresses squatted behind baskets of figs and dates, the empty dresses fluttering above them like the husks of former lives.

We walked behind a donkey laden with jerricans, deeper into the souk. The street was fecund with the odors of urine on stone, rank meat, old blood. A small boy cut in front of us, leading two brown-and-white sheep into a stall hung with hides and carcasses. The heads of other sheep regarded the new arrivals from copper trays, their necks cut ragged, their eyes heavy with useless wisdom.

The long tables inside Abu Shukairy's were lined with people hunched over their meals, eating as silently as if they were engaged in an act of prayer. At the counter near the entrance, the fat, happy man in a fez who was always there was pounding a heavy wooden pestle into a metal bowl of softened chick-peas, as he always did. He touched his fez in greeting.

There were two empty seats at one of the tables. As soon as we'd claimed them, a small boy came over and put down dishes of chopped onions, peppers, heated pita, and hommus. I mixed the onions into the hommus and began scooping it up. It was warm and delicious and I was glad to have something to do with my mouth. I didn't know what to say. My right hand was starting to hurt—it was a stupid way to hit someone. My knuckles were cut and swollen and the right side of my hand was still numb. I rubbed it, made more aware of it by Maryam's sidelong glances.

Drops of rain trailed down the panes of leaded glass that formed the front wall of the restaurant. They dappled the patrons' faces with gray, underwater shadows and made the room a closed, comfortable sanctuary.

"Who do you think those people were?" Maryam asked.
"Jews."

She shook her head disgustedly. "You don't think they were provocateurs, from the police or Shin Bet?"

"Don't be paranoid."

"Listen—" she started.

Whatever she was going to say was interrupted by a sudden crackle of static from outside. It broke into an amplified chant: the muezzin calling the faithful to prayer. Maryam went back to her food, pushing hommus over whatever she'd intended to say. We ate in silence again. A man at the other end of the table was explaining something in broken English to the couple sitting by him. He wore a keffiyeh and a white shirt and sounded like a guide. The man and the woman he was talking to were both nodding frantically at the guide's words: they had the stubbornly desperate eyes of guru seekers. They were middle-age but dressed younger, in some sort of matching jean outfits. I looked away from them and out through the open front door of the restaurant. Some Arabic letters had been crudely spray-painted on the opposite wall—PLO graffiti. The letters were streaking, elongating in the rain. Maryam followed my stare. Her eyes were suddenly wet. She touched her breasts, where the fat man had prodded them, and I felt something swell in my throat, some silent, answering grief.

"Shit," she said, echoing the fat man's comment to me, like a curse he'd left after himself. I reached over and traced the skin under her eyes, wiping the wetness. She turned her face away, a pressure of unspoken words twitching her mouth. "I thought I actually experienced the feeling," the woman at the other end of the table said in English to her guide, "of actually moving back into the first century." The guide picked up the nod: the three of them nodding eagerly, in throes of agreement. Maryam sighed, as if easing a weight off herself.

"What I started to say before was this—if you'd like to go out of town for a few days, why not come out to Jebel Halim? You've never seen our house."

I stared at her. "What would your mother say?"

She shrugged. "Oh, Aida will probably just put you to work."

"You didn't mention work."

Maryam broke off a piece of pita and ran it through the hommus.

"You work only if you want to." She pointed with the bread at her plate. "If you want to eat."

The projector threw a square of light on the screen and the film
began. A man grinned sardonically at an arched doorway.

"Riad Karaman," Elhannan muttered. "Aka George Yas-
sin and Yussef Biram."

"Watch," I said.

There was a sudden break in the film—perhaps the cameraman had feared being spotted. When Riad Karaman was
picked up again it was from a different angle. He was going
into the door.

"Do we have sound inside, Aharon?"

"Yes. I'll play the tape for you later."

People were passing the door without sound. Gliding. A
man in a pin-striped suit. Then Maryam Halim. She entered
the door of the restaurant.

"Stop here," I said. Elhannan turned off the projector. I
switched on the tape and let him listen.

"We have her, Aharon," he said when it was finished.

"We've had her for a long time."

"Do you want me to pick her up?"

I studied my assistant. The only time Elhannan allowed himself to register any emotion was at moments like this; he vibrated visibly with a repressed excitement, the slight speeding of pitch that could be felt in an instrument about to achieve the purpose for which it had been designed. I sometimes wished I could feel some affection for the boy: Elhannan was more my inheritor, my kaddish, than my own nephew. But I suppose it would be like feeling affection for a weapon, and I'd outgrown that sort of thing in my youth. *I kiss the two of you, my darling; my Kalashnikov and you.* "Like a rabbi," Yair, the Stern Gang leader, wrote:

> *who carries his prayer book in a velvet bag*
> *to the synagogue*
> *So carry I*
> *my sacred gun to the temple*

"And if we pick her up?" I asked. "What do we have?"

"A case. Consulting with a known PLO agent. Her connection to Karaman is solid now."

"We would have enough to give her a few years in Ramle," I said. "It isn't enough."

"It would normally be more than enough for you." Elhannan wagged his head slyly at me, an imitation of human movement he judged was appropriate. "Why is this Arab different from all other Arabs?"

"She's an Israeli citizen. We can't afford to let a trend get started. For one thing."

"For another, she has a relationship with your nephew."

I turned and looked at him. "Meaning what, Elhi?"

"She's an Israeli-Arab who can be connected to the terrorists. Who can be connected to Breira. You want to tie

Breira to her, let it fall with her. Do you think I'm too dense to see where you're going?"

Elhannan's face was closed with anger, but he was biting off his words, afraid of going too far. A young man who thought he had so much to lose. I wondered if his display of controlled anger was real or simply an imitation, another human trick Elhannan thought he was expected to perform—the old man likes passion and frankness, he'd been told. He stared at me coldly.

"Do you know what I am, Aharon? I'm the stranger claiming a position in the family firm that the owner wants for his own ungrateful son."

"Be patient," I said, with deliberate ambiguity, not explaining whether I was referring to his position or to Maryam Halim's arrest. Not letting my surprise at his perception show. He was right, of course. He was what I had now, Elhannan, the cold child of my old age.

"For how long?"

He wanted me to say it, put it into words.

"Listen to me closely," I said. "Get everything exactly right so that if it goes wrong you'll be able to repeat what I said and absolve yourself of any responsibility. Listen to me. I want you to let Maryam Halim fall until she's in deep enough so that we can punish her badly. This is too important to go any other way."

Elhannan nodded smoothly, his face bloating slightly with triumph.

"Is there anything else?" I asked.

"No, of course not." He wheeled around and left the room.

Leaving behind a note of disquiet in my breast, a momentary ache of doubt. How eager we'd been to create Elhannan. Disciplined, stolid, passionless, Jabotinsky's product of school and army camp. But of course it's Breira, that intense group of garrulous fanatics, that reminds me more than Elhannan of our younger selves, of the Yairs, the Hakims, the poetic killers. Like all fathers, we'd strived to destroy in our children what we despised in ourselves, and both where we succeeded and where we failed, we'd ended with children who despised us.

I opened my desk drawer and extracted the few "reports" Ezra had given me, papers I kept hidden, their existence as embarrassing as the bad poetry of my own youth. And more potentially damaging, if ever viewed by Elhannan: the old man has gone soft, indulgent. I wondered myself at keeping these documents, as if they were hostages, although I'd never try to blackmail Ezra with them. I could picture the look of self-righteous martyrdom that would blossom on his face: "Go ahead," he'd insist—like any of the tortured types I keep as informants, at least the better class of them, he's more than ready to be punished. I smoothed the papers under my fingertips, a light oil of sweat smearing the letters, bleeding them. He'd told me nothing I didn't already know, the useless information he'd given me fitted, as if mockingly, into what he imagined was the format of an intelligence report, as if to underscore to me that he understood what he was doing was merely symbolic, a demonstration of loyalty and commitment. What I saw as his perception, the game he played with me, had at first delighted me, as if it were an extension of the elaborate teasing he'd subjected me to when he was a child. But the format had slipped, the satire had worn thin, a note of hysteria and self-doubt had crept into the monologue, and what bled now under my fingers was my nephew himself.

Incident: November 11

Two truckloads of yeshiva students from the Rabbi Kruk Institute in Givat Sha'ul took over a few hills and someone's olive groves near Beit Hanina for a settlement. Set up an "overnight" tower and wall village, in imitation of the original Zionist pioneers. Breira called an emergency strategy situation. Deddy suggested that our slogan should be "If they take over other people's houses, we'll take over theirs." He had intelligence (see my report on Dov S., the religious boy who's a secret Breira member) that the yeshiva itself had been left mostly empty.

So we took over the building, marched into it singing pioneer songs with self-conscious irony. Deddy even put on a black robe and we sat around him like disciples around a dynastic holy man and engaged in an animated Talmudic discussion, rocking back and forth, giving questions and answers in whiny singsong. Of course the real yeshiva students soon got wind of what we'd done and hurried back to Jerusalem. There was fighting in the street in front of the building. Tanned secularists in jeans and work shirts pouring out of the yeshiva and battling pale yeshiva bochurs with whirling earlocks and yarmulkes who'd come from the wilderness. Like a civil war in our own psyches. For one moment everyone stopped and stared at one another in astonishment, for the space of a breath, as if the same vision had gathered in front of our eyes. But maybe it was just my imagination. Deddy was hit in the face with a brick.

Profile: Yael Ziegler

b. Jerusalem, 1949. Parents fought in the Belsky partisan group in White Russia. Currently own and operate an appliance store on Ben Yehuda Street. Apolitical. As if to say: "Enough." Their daughter's education includes a bagrut from the Rehavia Gymnasia and three years at Hebrew University, faculties: mathematics and philosophy. She's currently working toward a degree but is undecided in which discipline. Army service: active duty, 1967–68. Battalion clerk, Givati Brigade during the Six-Day War. Called to active reserve status during the 1973 war. Operations clerk, Schneller Barracks, Jerusalem. Highest rank: corporal. Apolitical until her brother David's death—he was wounded in the Sinai and succumbed at Shaare Zedek Hospital in Jerusalem, October 25, 1973. Became involved with Breira in 1975. Yael's politics are confused. She looks at the war as a mathematical formula that can, and therefore should, be solved; as a syllogism with clear premises and a forthright conclusion. She believes Breira's program, which emphasizes disregarding the "baggage of the past," i.e., the weight of remembered murders, allows movement toward that conclusion. At the same time, she cannot get rid of the baggage of her own past. Her hatred is a dead twin hanging around her neck, whispering mockingly into her ear, chuckling malevolently at the word "solution."

Report: 11/13

You complain that I don't give you anything of real value. You say you want more "flavor," an indication of both the "spirit and the substance" of the organization. You want, you say, "more details." Let me try to give you a picture then. Look. In this particular room are Yonatan Grossman, Avraham Bechor, Deddy Gur, Yael Ziegler. And me. Their chronicler. As others search the building, we sit behind the long tables the yeshiva students use as desks, sit on their benches, licking our wounds with smug pride. We've donned their black robes. Our faces look pale and severe, as if we've reverted to ancestral types. How easily we could be them. Deddy strolls in front of the classroom, bristling with energy, a fur-rimmed streimel askew on his head, a black robe open over his jeans and red plaid shirt. He thumbs with amazed delight a pile of books on the teacher's desk, holds up a pamphlet for us to see: it's one of ours. He picks up books, reads their titles, passes them to us. They aren't prayer books, or perhaps they are, the commentaries of a religion narrowed to its national base. Jabotinsky, Rav Kook, and Begin instead of Rashi and Maimonides. We open them, recite passages to one another in the singsong of prayer, rock back and forth on our heels. Yael sneers at us. I know what she means. This supercilious air about us, our attitude of being party to an inside joke annoys me. At the same time I feel very close to these people, as if they know my secrets. A civil war in my own psyche. The black shadow within. You would no doubt tell me that this is a natural feeling for somebody operating "undercover," a word you'd choose for its romantic connotations.

What do we talk about? What do you expect? Pilpul. Tactics, positions, the same never-ending drone of prayer.

Rabbi Yonatan: OK, so we take over a building, it's neat, we shine in the eyes of a few moderates and the Palestinians and the foreign press. But we're pissing away our moral advantage by being here. I still maintain that. Look, these people are a fringe, but a lot of people admire what they're doing. We have to ask why that is.
Rebbe Yael: Because of Arab intransigence.
Rabbi Yonatan: Exactly, in a way.
(Laughter)

Rabbi Deddy: We should adopt that as our slogan.

Rebbe Yael: I don't believe this. Look, they're on their way back and we're still in the ideological stage. What are we going to do? Deddy, take off that silly hat.

Rabbi Yonatan: Look, the fanatics are taking over more than land or a building. They're usurping an image, a national archetype that used to belong to the left. The pioneer—

Rabbi Deddy: With a gun and a plow. With a song in his heart and a tree in his hand. With all that crap. Only they uproot trees.

Rabbi Yonatan: But that's not what people see. They see familiar figures from their history lessons, from their parents' stories, from their own memories even, out creating a buffer zone for the country's greater security. Settling the land, in other words.

Rebbe Yael: And our greater security? What the hell are you rabbis doing? They'll be at the door soon.

Rabbi Avraham *(Nodding sagely):* While we're perceived as hooligans, defacing a religious institute.

Rabbi Deddy: They offer no real solutions.

Rabbi Yonatan: People see occupation as a real solution.

Rabbi Avraham *(Brandishing a book):* We shall make them hewers of wood and drawers of water.

Rabbi Deddy: Northern Ireland.

Rabbi Avraham: We shall form part of Europe's fortified wall against Asia and fulfill the role of cultural vanguard facing the barbarians.

Rabbi Deddy: Or South Africa.

Rebbe Yael: Deddy, stop rocking back and forth. You look like an idiot.

Rabbi Yonatan: People have an understandable aversion

to being the morally perfect victims that the world loves.

Rabbi Deddy: They need peace with security, but they also need to think about the quality of that peace. Now I sound like a fucking rabbi. *(He picks up a Breira pamphlet as if it's a Torah scroll, grins, chants Breira's Herzl.)* Zi-on-ism con-tains not on-ly the as-pi-ra-tion for a se-cure pi-ece of la-and for our un-for-tu-nate pe-o-ple, but also the as-pi-ra-tion for eth-i-cal and spir-i-tu-al per-fec-tion.

That's the Torah on one foot, he says. *Amen sela,* we say, swaying in rhythm along with him. They're going to shoot our ethical and spiritual asses, Rebbe Yael murmurs. We quote Rabbi Begin to her. We have to hate the horrifying, age-old, inexcusable, utter defenselessness of the Jewish people. Do not try to raise a hand against us or we will be forced to cut it off without delay by force of our arms. *Amen sela,* she says. Rabbi Weizmann has said: We Jews who aspire to rebuild our destroyed and dispersed people will respect and honor similar aspirations among other peoples, Rabbi Deddy insists. So I remember an old lady in the village of Beit Ikssa, how she wouldn't budge from her sofa so Deddy took one end and I took the other and we carried her out in the middle of her other stuff. Rabbi architect and rabbi policeman. I remember faces and stones. I remember the words you poured into my ears like sulfuric acid dripped at a controlled rate into fulminate while my father dozed in his chair. The sayings of the prophet Stern. Thus said Rabbi Yair. Your children will be orphans as you orphaned the children of Israel. For every cry of a boy from the top of a burning boat, for every cry of a Hebrew mother when her child embarks on a broken ship in the middle of the night—we shall answer you. We came in fire and we were burned, we came in water and we were drowned: we the remnants walk in rivers of blood, the blood reaches our necks, our mouths, our eyes, and from the fire and water and blood, trembling arms are raised, voices cry out, and from the mouths and eyes and from the trembling fingers, from the water and the fire and the blood, from there we are coming up, we are coming. Woe unto you.

But of course I said nothing. I was undercover.

Profile: Deddy Gur

b. Nahariya, 1947. Father from Romania, mother from Germany. Both parents illegal immigrants during the British Mandate who met on a blockade-running refugee ship. All other family members perished in Europe, in the usual manner, in fire and in blood. Parents moved to Jerusalem in 1950. Father presently retired projectionist, various cinemas (when we were kids, Aharon, he let Deddy and I come up in the booth with him, but only after he'd turned his girlie calendar to the wall). Mother, housewife. Apolitical. As if to say: Enough. Education: Bagrut, Beit Hakerem Gymnasia; engineering degree, Technion, 1971. Currently taking history degree, Hebrew University. Active military service, 1965–68. Officer course. Highest rank: captain. Combat service: 1967, Six-Day War (West Bank and Old City of Jerusalem). 1969–71 (as reserve officer): War of Attrition, Suez Canal. Occupation duty, West Bank and Gaza. Commanded unit involved in reprisal actions. 1973: mobilized on first day of

Yom Kippur War. Commanded unit involved in holding action on the Golan Heights. Wounded, traumatic amputation of left arm. Founded Breira peace group, 1974. I remember the exact day, if not the exact date, Aharon. He was still in the hospital and he conceived the idea of Breira after seeing a documentary on the ward TV about American war veterans throwing their medals away. "I had a Demerol vision," he said to me. And then we argued. But I hadn't taken him seriously, not until I was in Germany and read about the group he'd started. The idea of Israeli soldiers protesting their war caught the German imagination—it was a cover story in *Stern*—but then the Germans always enjoy news like that. Every time a house is blown up on the West Bank or an old lady carried out on a sofa it's front-page news, as if to say: You see, they do it too.

So what else can I tell you about my friend Deddy, Uncle Aharon? Clowns simplify in order to demonstrate absurdity. In this light, Deddy's politics are deliberately simplified, Tolstoyan: he concentrates, as he says, on the basics of the situation and doesn't allow himself to be sidetracked by the baggage of the past, that dead twin we all have hanging around our necks. Is this really of some use to you, Aharon? Do I really need to reiterate this? But you asked, so I did. That's the Torah on one foot.

I put his Torah down on my desk. Commentaries and dialogues, the pilpul he'd reported within himself, this hodgepodge record of a lost soul done in good police format. The report I had from Elhannan (he'd carried it personally to my office, placed it without comment on my desk) about Ezra's action against Yoram Romano at the Breira rally was merely a final comment, his punch to Romano's face merely an ending punctuation mark, a final welt he'd written on my heart. The gray stolidity of the bulked objects around me seemed suddenly weightless, their weight flowing from them, the cocoon I'd constructed in this building of cocoons, the self I'd created to be a buffer between myself and the real world, to allow me to operate in it, suddenly unweaving, pulling some comforting mass of weight from me that flew away lightly as a soul and I felt reamed and empty.

I fluttered my fingers over the reel and allowed myself to retreat from the gathered stillness of my office, my cell across from the building where the British once held me in a cell. From the silent monuments of my file cabinets, from the dead, cyclopean eye of the projector. Retreat to where? Of course to those Friday night dinners together at my brother's house, the three of us: the bachelor, the widower, and the child who was our pivot. *Aba* and *aba,* daddy and daddy, Ezra called us: there would have been no table between my brother and me if not for him. But there had been no table, no Shabbat dinners: apparently those evenings had no resonances; they never existed; they're merely part of the baggage of the past. No cholent and sweet wine, no grapefruit juice for Ezra (or for the Halim children, when they came. Or didn't come). No stringy chicken overcooked by that strange pair of parents, my brother and I. No candy the boy would search for in my pockets, sweets I would put there to sweeten my entrance, like a rabbi placing a dab of honey on a child's prayer book to sweeten the words. Once, when Ezra was a baby, I even dabbed my fingers into the honey pot and let him lick them, so he'd lick sweetness and not the taste of blood from my hands. But that bad youthful poetry never happened, did it? There was no challah or music or stories, those tales headier than even the Red Indian tales Ezra loved. But your stories are true, *aba* and *aba,* he'd say, excitement trembling in his eyes like pieces of heated wire, and my brother and I would beam, seeing our past given meaning and connection and coherence by the child: two foolish vampires leeching on his sense of wonder at those tales of the fathers from the fathers. But they never happened. That table never existed. There were no stories. No moonless nights and signal fires answered by blinking flashes, no rafts on the beach. No baggage from the past with tattooed numbers on skeletal arms tottering toward us from the waves. They've all turned into comic, jerky figures that move too fast on a worn and grainy old film, with all their quaint sand kissing and obligatory horas. My brother and his mother and Amnon Sapir never danced with me and with my second, my Polish smuggler Nathan, a pirate Ezra loved to hear about, as if Nathan were one of his Cooper redskins. No mad socialists dancing with mad revisionists. None of us doing our trite dance with those skeletal Yids, those dead we pulled from the sea. From the fire and the blood and the water. Those walking dead and the reason they were there, yes, the fire they came from and the blood they came from and the water they came from, which never happened. Where did they go? They never existed. None of it happened.

It all never happened, did it, Ezra? You never sat at that table and listened with wonder, my dear nephew, my own ungrateful son, my kaddish. But you know, like a welt on your own heart, that what's missing from the clean mathematical formula is precisely that baggage from the past. That baggage from the sea. That sea lapped beneath our Shabbat table, and our Shabbat table shimmers beneath the words in your reports; it serves up a civil war in your own psyche. Those nonexistent wraiths and archetypes you write about who came from water and blood and fire and currently own and operate an appliance store on Ben Yehuda. That black shadow that moves within you, that baggage you wrote of who perished in the usual manner, who met on a blockade-running refugee ship moored in your mind from our table, our tales, the explosive mixture I, yes, poured into your ears, yes, a debt hissing like acid in your ear. Yael's dead brother? What about your own mother? Hannah deposits you on the earth like a replacement and a month later she's gone. Profile: Ezra Brenner. b. 1947, Jerusalem. Participant with honor in all the usual wars. Father, Amos, and mother, Hannah, originally refugees from the Russian-Polish Pale, a buffer zone that offered no buffer. Cofounders, Kibbutz Beit Haharim. Very political. Cofounders, Arab-Jewish Peace League, 1934. Young men and women with burning eyes and disheveled hair and short-term memories extending the fragile crystal of peace in their trembling hands. To have it knocked to the ground like a Coke bottle. Because there was no answer, no Arab Breira, no one home. Mother's military service: Palmach. Killed at the battle for Castel. During a war that her Arab brothers and sisters began after they'd been given territorial compromises and still weren't nudged to be reasonable, after they'd been given two-thirds of our land as a gift and had something to lose and still wanted everything. Do I really need to reiterate this to you, Ezra? But you ask, so I will. Do you cover your hand with honey and extend it to a rabid dog? To maniacs who lick our blood? To, in a phrase, human beings like us? That's the Torah on one foot. And while we're at it, what do you see in this girl? Some secret about yourself? A pot of honey you want to dip your own bloody fingers into? Are you mad? And if you are, kaddish, what do I have? Elhannan? Where are you going with this?

. . . . .EZRA

I went out to Jebel Halim the next afternoon. The rain that had started the day before was still falling. It beat on the roof of the Land-Rover, let off, trailed into a beading mist as I drove down the muddy, puddle-pocked main street of the village. The stone houses on each side of me pressed in and seemed to give off a subtle, intimate heat. I drove past the open door of a teahouse. Inside, a circle of young men were playing shesh besh, their breath floating in broken spider threads above the playing boards. They turned to stare at me and their faces became hard and blank.

The street turned into a narrow mud path and began to slope up steeply. It continued past the last houses of the village, then farther up, up to the cap of the hill on which Jebel Halim was built. As I climbed higher, the countryside came into view. The row of bare hills that lay between Jerusalem and Jebel Halim were circled with the traces of ancient terraces, like lines on a topographic map, the buildings over in the city flat and gold against a watercolor gray sky. It started to rain again.

Near the crest, the path veered to the left, following the ridge line. A house came into view just below me, growing out of the slope that faced the city. It was clean lined and nicely simple, built of solid, fitted blocks of hand-chiseled, pink-hued Jerusalem stone. A dome grew from the house as naturally as the house grew from the hill, more weathered than the rest of the house, constructed of smaller bricks that glistened wetly, their outlines clear in the rain, and at their apex the keystone, the rock that braided the entire dome together, that if shattered would bring it all down. From the angle of the path I could see down to the fig and olive trees spaced neatly on the flank of the hill below the house, their roots muscling fetidly out of the earth. Beyond the building, wigging the hill, was a grove of oak and pine trees, their branches stirring uneasily, as though they'd recognized sergeant architect.

I parked in front of the house and got out. The door was framed by the same large, chiseled stones, laid counter to the other stones, a blessing in Arabic filigreed into the top row. The door opened and Maryam looked out, smiling at me.

"Why are you standing in the rain?"

She took my overnight bag. I left my shoes in the hallway and followed her into a large central room, its ceiling the underside of the high dome. Aida Halim was standing in the center of the room like an exhibit, tall and willowy in a long, blue-dyed village dress that seemed a costume on her: I remembered her as always being in Western dress. In some ways she looked to have aged less than Maryam: with the years a strength had blossomed on her face, opening it.

"Welcome, Ezra. It's good to see you again." Aida took my hands and kissed me on both cheeks.

Maryam stepped up next to her. "Would you like some

coffee?" she asked. Arabs and Jews and cakes and grapefruit juice. Before I could answer, she'd left the room.

It was a room comfortable as a good memory: furnished with stuffed chairs covered by flower patterns and a large sofa and low tables inlaid with Bethlehem mother-of-pearl and a deep blue Isfahan carpet. There were niches in the stone walls, a television sitting in one like a squat household god and shelves set neatly in others, stacked with books, with copper Arab knickknacks and framed photos, one of Shahid and Maryam and me, a clutter that annoyed me so that my eyes fled up the wall to more framed photos—Shahid and Walid Halim, set high up on the white, laundress's blue-tinted limewash of the wall, set in the old style, for a time when one sat lower to the floor and one's line of vision went naturally higher.

Aida knelt smoothly in front of two kerosene heaters, priming them as if performing a ritual of hospitality.

"I didn't realize it was so cold in here," she said apologetically. "We were in the kitchen. And it takes so long to heat this room." She gestured up at the dome. "This was the only part of the house that was still standing when we came here. We've been rebuilding the rest of the house around it."

They'd left the domed room open, in the traditional style, and I thought how it had changed in the homes that I'd entered in the villages, their space no longer open, but subdivided into small, tight rooms, partitioned, schizophrenic, a problem in clean collapses; even the sensuously curved underside of the arch, the secret part of the house, hidden from the eyes of the dwellers, as if they were ashamed of looking at their own nakedness. And then I thought how the model that I carried in my mind, the keystone that braided me to a profession, a vocation too holy to ever obtain, was the open-domed ceiling and vaulting walls of the Halim house in Jerusalem and how I hadn't known until now that it had been but an echo of a memory, an echo of this house.

The small nets on the heaters began glowing deep red, playing on Aida's face, softening it into a calmer, gentler archetype of Maryam's face, one kept hidden at home, in one of the niches in the wall.

"How do you pay for it?" I asked.

Aida chuckled and stood up. "The famous Israeli bluntness. I miss it, in this oblique world. I miss it—sometimes. We're still living on my husband's death, Ezra. His insurance, his land, his house, the royalties from his writing, his name. We're still living on his death and we're still hated for his life. That's how we pay for it." She smiled wryly. "When visiting him in the hospital, Walid would whisper to me that his relatives had put all their hate into his liver."

"But you still stay here."

"It's insane, isn't it?"

She spread her hands in amazement, as if helpless against her own irrationality. She'd been known, according to my father, for her glittering social salons in the days before the state. I couldn't imagine her life here. Or perhaps I could, too well. But it had been her choice and my sympathy was for the daughter in whose vaulting, open mind narrow partitions had been erected, partitions that only loud bangs, the noises of a child who'd been ignored, could bring down.

"After a while we became more accepted." Aida nodded to herself. "It's a matter of not being blunt, of knowing the patterns. Also, my husband's brother is mukhtar now: his friendship has helped."

There was a clatter in the kitchen, a pot or pan falling, and we both looked toward the noise.

Aida said, "Maryam made her own private attempt at reassimilation last year, when she got back from the States."

"How was that?"

"Oh, she got herself engaged to a cousin of ours from Amman, from my husband's side. It was her idea of back to tradition. Tradition was a fat Jordanian businessman she'd never met. But in the end she changed her mind."

"And broke it off?"

Aida looked at me strangely.

"A few days before the wedding was to take place she made up a story. It was about you."

I waited, but she didn't go on.

"I'd like to hear it."

Aida shook her head. "I don't know why she came up with it. Apparently you were still living in her mind. She told her fiancé that she had once 'gone out' with a Jewish boy named Ezra Brenner. What is this 'going out'? he asked. Then he declared the only way for the wedding to go through would be for Maryam to go to Hadassah Hospital and get a certificate of virginity. Hadassah does such things, you know—they love to do such things for us."

"What did she do?"

"It's what I did, Ezra. I went back to tradition myself. I told him to take his feet and run or I'd have my relatives here kill him. And you know, I would have too," Aida said blandly, "but the fat pig saw that and ran back to Amman."

She smoothed the front of her dress as if soothing herself.

"I haven't seen you in years," I said slowly. "And now the first thing you think to tell me about is this."

"Yes? What are you asking?"

"Why?"

"So that you know. Come, let's eat."

She and Maryam had prepared a kibbeh of grilled lamb and saffron rice. As we sat down, Maryam produced two dusty bottles of slivovitz from behind her back with a magician's flourish. The two of us looked at each other and laughed.

"I kept them as souvenirs," Maryam said.

"I don't remember us stealing that many."

Maryam put the bottles on the table and touched each lightly. "Shahid's theory was that it must be weak, like fruit juice, because of the little picture of the plum on the label."

Aida was staring at us, her eyebrows raised. "What is this?" she asked, and I explained. One year my father had insisted on having the Halims over to celebrate the Passover with us. After the seder, Shahid and I—we must have been about fourteen years old—had filched several bottles of slivovitz from the liquor cabinet and he, Maryam, and I had gone up to the Halims' roof, where the two of us had gotten vomiting drunk on a half a bottle while Maryam laughed at us.

"I thought you were the funniest things I'd ever seen," she said.

I glanced at Aida, trying to gauge her reaction to the story, to the mention of Shahid. She picked up one of the bottles and studied it, then unscrewed the cap and filled her glass and ours.

"I remember the seder," she said. "You have no idea how upset your father was, Ezra. He'd told Walid and me that the words of the service had become a meaningless drone to him, as prayers do; he hadn't realized how they would sound to our ears. We told him not to be silly, that we appreciated his sensitivity, and we did, Ezra, but his choice of discussing it, of bringing it out, made us even more uneasy. Shahid felt it; he always felt it more than you or Maryam.''

Maryam raised her glass, held up a jagged piece of pita in her other hand. "This is the bread of affliction," she intoned. "All who are in need, let them come and celebrate the Passover. Now we are here—next year we shall be in the land of Israel. Now we are slaves—next year we shall be free. *Le-shana ha'ba'a b-Yerushalayim.* Next year in Jerusalem.''

"Next year in Switzerland," I said, toasting her.

"So says the simple son." She clicked my glass and we drank. Aida looked at us thoughtfully. The smoky, bittersweet taste of the brandy and the remembered rhythms of the seder tapped open other images in my mind.

"Do you remember our football games? The chanting about killing the Arab when Shahid would come out onto the field?''

Maryam nodded. "Whenever Shahid would play, I'd stand on the YMCA balcony with my father and chant 'Kill the Jews' under my breath until he made me stop.''

"Those Kurds we played with were rough boys—they spread it around that they'd take care of anyone who called Shahid names, and it stopped.''

"Unless he didn't play well," Aida said.

I grinned at her. "Then they'd chant it themselves.''

They hesitated a moment, and then we all laughed. A steady, lulling patter beat on the domed roof like an echoing of it, an extension of the sense of peaceful closure that was flowing suddenly from the table. The room felt close and comfortable, insulated in a larger dome of sound, woven to the keystone of memory that bound us together and existed in spite of anything I'd done and allowed forgiveness, allowed me back inside a place to which I'd thought I could never return. I couldn't think of any place I'd rather be. Gusts of wind rattled the window.

Something crashed through one of them. Glass fountained toward me, glittering shards of it hanging suspended like a shattering of the air and of time and in that suspension was the thought that this was finally what it was like, to be inside, and I was on my feet, rage at this violation of the fragile structure we'd constructed pushing me to the front door. I flung it open. A rock smashed into the wall near my face. I snarled into the darkness. Aida came out and took my arm. I shook her off and stepped farther outside.

The wind tore at my hair. It was pitch black. I could see nothing. The moon showed for an instant, and then I could see the trees in the grove on top of the hill, their trunks half lit and twisted, their leaves shaking violently, as if an electric current were running through them. Aida and Maryam were both standing next to me.

"It's just the neighbors," Aida said.

. . . . .AIDA

At last they were asleep and the house was quiet. I went to the kitchen and dried the dishes. The faucet was dripping, a soft drip, but constantly there: my senses fibered to the house. I couldn't hear the boy's breathing, but I could feel it: an ever so slight increase in the emanations and pressures of the house, a tickling against my exposed nerves, an imbalance in my sense of myself, as when I had children growing in my womb. As a child he'd been all dark, hungry eyes and bony knees, as if his father had produced a refugee, a physical representation of all the emaciated concentration camp children that he couldn't save, that he held in his mind. Next to him, growing up, my Shahid looked like a robust sabra. The boy upstairs, I'd thought. He was no longer a boy. And he'd never looked like Shahid, and if Shahid were his age now they still wouldn't look alike. He was a stranger in my house, an imbalance. My husband, watching the three of them playing together in the white dust of our courtyard, would gush at the similarities he forced himself to see—he'd carve the flesh of my children into a poem.

How alike they seem, clear-eyed and tanned
pale scholars and fellahin
years of conflict coming to a sun-blessed resolution in their flesh.

The boy, the man, upstairs, had his father's tallness and darkness, his father's bony knees and lean question of a body, but I saw, in the quick turn of his head, in the sharp knives of his eyes, in the tousled curls of his hair, more of Aharon. Aharon in the leather jacket he always wore when I first met him, sweating under it in the summer heat of Jerusalem, a damp curl of hair over his forehead: the picture of a man affecting the appearance of a young revolutionary, but one knew he was actually a daydreaming store clerk and that was his disguise. His eyes smoldering with disdain, darting about the walls of my house, weakening them with cracks of contempt. His brother in his khaki shorts, his white, bony knees open and friendly, twinkling. How glad they were to finally meet the charming wife of Walid Halim. The poet and his lovely wife, Jerusalem's most famous hostess. How much we have in common, as your husband so courageously writes. How silly to allow British imperialism to turn us against each other when we are sons of the same Semitic family. Poets and warriors and scholars. My husband gazing into his coffee cup, tilting it back and forth between his thumb and forefinger and smiling as if he could discern a bright future in its depths. Cool, but touched in his heart they'd come. Flattered by his words in their mouths.

When they'd gone, I'd taken the cups to the sink and they'd already been mixed so I didn't know which of the two brothers had left the folded piece of paper in one. *My love put his hand through the grill and set my bowels aching for him. I rose up to let my love in with my hands all sticky with myrrh.* I'd felt nothing but a mild sense of amusement. I was used to flirtations, crushes. Jerusalem's most famous hostess. I was used to British matrons gushing at me, their Arab friend in her long, beautifully embroidered "village" dress, fixing pictures in their minds of themselves standing next to me: their memories the booty they'd carry back to their cold, less clean, less green land. I was used to being representative: the Christian girl my husband courted fiercely for five years, braving the objections of his family and my own, objections sometimes couched in bullets. Chipping away at the walls of prejudice until he'd obtained me, to place me in his house, up on his shelves with his books about Arab unity. I was used to it, but I still wondered what elusive triumph I could represent to Amos Brenner—for I could only imagine his kindly, hairy knees when I saw those few lines of poetry.

I spilled a pile of beans out of the bag I'd bought in the Old City that morning onto the table. A deliberate gesture of sympathetic magic. Of memory. Of mourning. I began scooping the beans into the grinder. The released smell of coffee sweetened the air. I ran my fingers through the pile of beans, seeking their hidden warmth, seeking my memories.

There was a fig tree in our courtyard in Jerusalem, its leaves covered with a white dust that aged and mocked their dangling male shapes. I could see it from our kitchen window. Blue curtains, faded in the sun, snapping light and air into the kitchen, light and air from the north, from the Old City, air dry and sharp with heat and the scent of dust and olive wood. The black shadows of branches moving silently on the white wall across from me. When my house in Jerusalem had been around me, a shell of white brightness and heat and my unconceived children stirring in me like shadows on a wall and a pile of coffee beans on the table also. And there'd been a knock on the door.

There'd been a knock on the door and I'd answered it and he'd stood there, an uncertain smile twisting his lips, the black curl of hair flipped deliberately, I was sure, over his forehead, the brown leather jacket in spite of the heat. A fierce masculine smell of leather and sweat and force intruding into the morning of my house.

"My husband is at the YMCA," I'd said to Aharon Brenner.

"There's something I must tell you."

"I'll call him."

"There's no need."

He stepped closer to me, a strong smell of sweat wafting from the open collar of his shirt.

"This afternoon," he said, "whatever happens, stay in your house. But leave all of your windows open."

He looked at me, that querulous smile trembling on his lips. Waiting for my questions. Why have you told me? he wanted me to say. Thank you, he wanted me to say. He'd rehearsed our dialogue, scripted our conversation: my responses, his replies, in his mind. I said nothing.

"Do you know the risk I'm taking, coming here?"

"I'll call my husband."

"Later," he said, his voice hoarse. He tried to smile again, his face wet, the curled hair of his chest exposed and obscene, dripping. Later, he said, dismissing Walid, as if my husband was without seriousness or force, a boy, a woman, and I understood what brings women to occupiers. He touched my shoulder, then gripped it painfully, pushing in, intruding, trapping me with his weight, his force. I grabbed a handful of beans from the table and threw them in his face. He pushed me away and shook his head, the small smile still

on his lips, as if it were a bemused spectator to the actions
of his body.

"I'm sorry," he said. "I'm terribly sorry."

I said nothing. A few of the coffee beans had stuck to the
wetness of his face. He wiped them off, shrugging.

"Whatever happens," he said, "stay inside. Stay away
from the hotel. Stay off Julian Way."

I stayed inside. I called Walid and he came home and
opened all of the windows, though when I told him to call
the police, he refused. They honor us, he said. A blow against
imperialism, he said. His words were like words in a foreign
tongue to me. I turned from him and looked out of the window I'd just opened. Parked in the alley between our house
and the French Consulate was a blue taxi, the man in its
driver's seat wearing a brown leather jacket. Hunched over
the wheel. Waiting.

We went upstairs to our bedroom and piled a rampart of
cushions and pillows at the head of the bed and Walid and I
lay on our stomachs all the rest of that morning, watching
through the window so that when the shooting began it was
as if we were watching a cinema in the square of the window
frame. Arabs with guns bursting from the back of the hotel
basement. British soldiers chasing them. The Arabs turning
and firing machine guns. Stens, Walid whispered, his breath
hot in my ear: the Irgun weapon. Jews dressed as Arabs, he
whispered, as though it were an honor. An "Arab" falling
forward dramatically and his companion turning and throwing a cylinder that landed and rolled along the pavement
spewing dark smoke, and he grabbed the wounded man,
helping him with one arm, the two Irgunists firing through
the smoke, and the blue taxi suddenly in the picture, squeal-
ing to a stop next to them, the two men jumping in, the tires
screeching in the best cinematic fashion, Aharon's form

hunched over the wheel, his face looking up at me; the Tommies, their white knees exposed under their baggy comedians' khaki shorts, fanning out, firing after the car, and the smell of smoke intruding, destroying the cinema screen, into my house, acrid and stinging in my nostrils so that I pulled my husband to me, touching him wantonly, shamelessly, as I never had before, his mouth gaping and his eyes closed as we fumbled our clothing aside, the sweat on my husband's body acrid with the stink of cordite and smoke from outside and I licked it and he entered me, his semen tainted with Aharon's smoke.

And later, when the big blast had rocked our house and thrown dishes and books and knickknacks from the shelves, thrown the order from our house, later, in spite of Walid's imprecations—for what did they mean to me, from this man who couldn't protect me?—later, I went to Julian Way. I walked down the street I'd walked down every day of my life in Jerusalem and saw how the seeds placed in the basement of the hotel had become heat and pressure and stink, become a terrible masculine force that blew the roof away and the pillars of the basement from which we'd seen the terrorists run and pancaked the six floors of the hotel and the building had birthed a placenta of jagged chunks of concrete and broken glass and crude human forms out into Julian Way. So I walked down the street I'd walked every day of my life in Jerusalem, past the deformed children of the man who'd handed me a love poem that told me how I was to act, past smoking debris, overturned buses and cars, bodies licked by flames, and this is what I saw. Halfway up the wall of my husband's YMCA building, I saw the staring head of a man, stuck like a grotesque ornament, a bright red smear below it, streaking the wall, and I turned away and on the sidewalk near my feet I saw the face of a girl, peeled off and thrown down like a discarded rubber mask, elongated terribly: a face turned into a scream. Then a siren wailed as if coming from those two terrible mouths, and I felt the hot dust and ashes at my feet, Aharon's dust, enter me with that scream and those faces and I knew I'd conceived twins, the children of that day.

. . . . MARYAM

A patch of sunlight moving onto my pillow woke me. I lay in its warmth, stretching slowly, reluctant to get up. I could hear stirrings from the room next to mine where Ezra was. Creaks, rustles, a soft, protesting groan. I rose in a defiant flurry of energy and went to the window. There was a bruise of clouds to the west, but otherwise the sky was hard blue, clear. The village was laid out below in patterns of bright white squares and black shadow squares. Crescent curves gleamed off domed roofs in bazaar merchants' smiles, large and false. I leaned out and I could see the domes and cubes of Jerusalem cresting the high ridge line to the south, like the village's echo, or its source.

I dressed and went downstairs. The house was cool and quiet with shadows. The light coming through the kitchen window touched a silver glitter off the coffee grinder and woke the objects on the shelves: cans and jars and bottles. There was a plastic bag containing freshly ground coffee on the table. I filled the coffeepot with water, measured in coffee, and put it on the stove. I watched until it began to perk, standing still for a long time, letting the morning touch me. Ezra came into the room.

"You're up early," I said.

"I never sleep late."

We sounded like a language lesson. The coffee was perking madly. I took it off the fire and turned off the stove.

"Will you have a cup?"

"Thank you."

The pen of my aunt. Ezra's face was still puffy with sleep, vulnerable, his eyes etched around with smile or worry lines, little creases of white. I held down an impulse to reach over and trace them, the way he'd touched my face yesterday. I poured the coffee.

"I'd better leave today before you lose any more windows," Ezra said.

"Don't talk nonsense. You'd offend Aida."

"Would I offend you?"

I tossed my head. "I was going for a walk—would you like to come along?"

He hefted his cup, as if weighing my words. Say yes, I thought. Say no. Go away, fade back into my adolescence, become a gawky wonder again.

"Yes, why not?"

A warm breeze, heavy with the smell of pine and thistle, was blowing strongly outside, like the first, fast scout of a new season. The breeze pressed my dress against the back of my legs, stirred the small nest of hair on the back of my neck. I wished I hadn't pinned my hair up. My neck and back felt exposed as nakedness to the man behind me. The morning touched my skin as if it had been scraped down to my raw nerves. Ezra came up next to me, taking a deep breath of the air.

"A day like kisses on a wound," I said.

And wanted to fling myself off the side of the hill, disappear into a void. But he only smiled.

"That sounds like it should be part of an old Arab proverb."

"It almost is—it's a line from one of my father's poems."

"I read some of his work, in translation."

I searched his face for a hint of patronization or disdain. He smiled at me innocently.

"It doesn't translate well," I said. "The bird of justice beating its wings against the barred windows of my cell, all of that. It reads all right in Arabic, but not in Hebrew—it's too direct, too didactic. Most Israeli writers go the other way about the conflict. They'll only deal with it indirectly, through allegories, symbolism."

"Why mention it? It's a given—like the weight of the atmosphere on your skin."

The Israeli expert on everything. "Yes, I suppose that's true," I snapped. "In a country where every would-be architect is also a literary critic."

Ezra laughed. "As a would-be architect it bothers me that our architecture goes in the other direction. Our buildings are either Miami Beach or brutally obvious. We're here, they say. Like us or not."

"And what sort of buildings will you make?"

"I used to think I knew."

We were walking into the grove, the trees suddenly surrounding us. I saw Ezra looking around carefully, as if searching for ambushes or avenues of retreat. It was a soldier's look that annoyed me, here, on my ground.

"We wouldn't be bothered in the daylight," I said.

We were almost in the center of the grove now, the Jebel Halim oak coming into view. The grove has been here as

long as the village: both went back to biblical times and
perhaps before—this high ground had probably been a Ca-
naanite holy place. The oak, towering and alien, always
seemed to me to lay claim to a different kind of power than
that of the looming hills—a sly, poking quality, that of a
smaller, more intimate god. My own. Twice, in the last six
years, people had tried to burn it down, as if they were still
at war with the original deities of the land. I was at the tree
now. I lay my forehead against the char of the burn, pressing
hard into it. Protect me from the stranger, from the breezes
of the morning inside of me, from ambushes: show me avenues of retreat. I could feel the imprint of the burn being
pushed into my skin. When I came away, Ezra was looking
at me, the breeze rumpling his dark hair like a blessing, moving a ripple of gold along the lighter hair on his forearms.
He placed his hands on both sides of the oak, measuring it,
trying to possess it.

"Would you have been married here?"

I laughed, startled. Cursing Aida in my mind.

"No, of course not."

We would have been married in the village. The young
men would have erected a tent outside my uncle's house.
They would have stood in a line before it, singing my praises
while I listened from a room upstairs, contemplatively, mod-
estly. They would have set my bridegroom in a chair in the
middle of the tent, then painted his hand with henna, as if
he'd pulled out the blood of my virginity. Amid wild ulu-
lations I'd have been brought to him and white-headdressed
riders on gleaming white horses would have galloped around
us, authentic as hell. But the insight in Ezra's words shook
me. Could he see that clearly into me, see what this place
was to me? I'd brought him here as if I were introducing

him: here he is, the boy I told you about, what do you think? I touched the burn marks, the hard, ugly ridges of them, and shuddered.

"Come away from here, Ezra. Come, let's sit down someplace."

I led him to the south side of the grove, and we sat on the crest of the hill, facing the city. Pieces of rusting metal were scattered among the rocks below: a wrecked car—a Fiat, wheels gone, windows out—sat halfway down the slope, abandoned in 1967 by a family that had decided not to live under the Jews, not to make my father's decision. I threw a rock at it. The stone bounced off the hood.

I picked up another one and weighed it in my hand. Ezra was staring at the city. I followed his gaze. The older buildings looked bleached, faded in the strong light, but the newer structures—the high rises on French Hill, the faceted beehive tower of the Hilton—stood forward, claiming attention. We're here, like it or not. I threw the rock in their direction. I was aware of Ezra's hip, touching my own, but I didn't move. He was here, like it or not. And I didn't move. The clouds I'd seen threatening earlier were starting to crowd in from the west. Patches of white fog were moving in over the hills, drawing around them like curtains. Ezra stretched, the movement of his body consciously or unconsciously imitating the slow, encompassing motion of the fog. He pointed at the hilltop village it had just engulfed.

"Once, back before the last war, there were three brothers from Nebi Samwil who killed a Jewish motorist who'd given them a lift. Two held him and the third strangled him. What was strange about it was how they were caught. Their mother overheard them bragging about the killing, and then she saw a picture of their victim in the newspaper. It seems she'd once been a wet nurse for a Jewish family. The baby she'd nursed, who'd shared her breasts with her sons, had grown up to be murdered by them. When she recognized the name, she went a little mad and called the police."

"I remember that," I said.

"What I always wondered though, is if her sons knew who the man they killed was," Ezra went on. "The papers never said. Anyway, the police tried to keep quiet about who told them, but the news got out. Before they could act, put the mother into protective custody, she was killed by someone in the village."

I looked at him. "Why are you telling me this . . . fable?"

"I was on reserve duty at the time. My unit was sent there." He waved at the fog that covered Nebi Samwil. "The woman's house, of course, went to her sons after her death. Only it didn't. We blew it up. I blew it up. That was my job in the army, between wars—demolitions. Because of my architectural training, my knowledge of structures. That was the first time, though not the last." He jabbed at the fog. "Biddu. Beit Surik. Beit Ikssa. I could go on—those were just around here. And each time, I thought about your house in Jerusalem."

I moved away, hardening against him, a feeling I clung to like a refuge. "Is that what we are to you—some cheap redemption? Did you come out here to be part of another fable?"

His eyes flicked to mine, held my stare. He shrugged. "Isn't that why you invited me?"

"I invited you because I saw someone who needed a vacation. An old friend who looked lost and who'd helped me."

He reached over and touched my face, like a wisp of fog.

Like a kiss on a wound. "Maybe," he said. "Or maybe I want a place that's exempt from the law of gravity, outside the weight of the atmosphere. Maybe I want to step out of the fable." He opened his hands, as if releasing a bird.

"There's no such place," I said. I got up and brushed myself off, then started back through the trees, my pace quickening as I went, as if I were trying to outrun myself.

The day Ezra and I sat on the ridge seemed the edge of seasons. By the next morning the rain had stopped and it didn't start again. Around the village, the bare, dun-colored hills were gradually blurred with green and brightened by swaths of scarlet anemones and yellow cyclamens, their colors hopefully exaggerated by the translucent, magnifying air. The stone throwers didn't bother us again. I started going to my classes, but Ezra seemed content to drift with the changes in the country around us. He made no move to return to the city, and Aida made no hint that he should leave. She put him to work, as I'd promised him, laying flagstones for a patio that he designed. He mixed cement and lifted stones for hours without a break. I watched him sweating in the sun, his skin covered with the dust of stones, with the ghosts of stones.

To my astonishment, he began getting up early and running, following circular routes into the hills around the village, working up their steep flanks and along the deep-cut wadis until he knew a number of ways back to the Jebel

Halim grove, where he always ended his run. I watched him from my window. A small, white figure, darting here and there, systematically learning the geography that surrounded me.

One morning I overslept and was awakened by the sound of a motor being started under my window. I dressed and went downstairs, calling for Aida, but the house was empty. When I went outside, I saw Ezra tinkering under the hood of his car. He raised his head, then smeared a grease stain across his cheek.

"Good morning. Aida said to tell you she went to see your uncle." He closed the hood. "Listen, I'm going to get washed up, then drive into town to pick up some food for the house."

"Don't be silly."

"I've been eating here for a week." He held up his hand to stop my objections. "Look, I need to pick up some clothing too. Why don't you come along?"

"I don't think so."

"Come."

He closed the hood, as if finalizing it.

In the city, we drove to Beit Hakerem and parked by the supermarket at Denmark Square. Ezra pushed a cart down the aisles, grinning at me as if to say: Look at the two of us, playing house. I overshopped happily. At the checkout counter I told him to let me pay for at least half. He counted out his money, without replying.

Outside, I waved at the abstract statues of Jewish refugees and Danish boats engaged in saving same behind the park benches.

"Go ahead and get your clothing—I'll wait for you here."

"What are you afraid of, Maryam? Come."

"I just think it will be better if I wait here."

"Come."

The apartment he brought me to was in a different neighborhood from the apartment he'd lived in when we were young, but everything inside was the same, as if brought forward in a capsule. Stepping into it was like stepping into a part of my girlhood. Leather chairs and sofa, walls lined with dark-stained oak bookcases, their shelves tight with books; a huge silver samovar in one corner like a family shrine, and on one wall the real shrine—a portrait of Ezra's mother, Hannah. There was a fragile air of civilization about it that lingered in my nostrils like the memory of a musty odor. We're here, if you please.

"Do you want something to drink?" Ezra asked. "Coffee or tea?"

"Tea. I'll make it."

"Sit."

He put a record on the stereo, then went into the kitchen. Shostakovich—his father's music. It filled the apartment like his father's ghost.

The strains of the symphony were jarred by a knocking at the door. Ezra hurried out of the kitchen. When he walked back into the living room, he was followed by a stocky man in an open-necked white shirt and baggy khaki trousers. For a second I was startled: Ezra had reached again into the magic bag of his past and pulled out Amos Brenner. But this man was shorter, heavier; Amos's wild tufts of hair carefully cropped and held tightly in control.

Then I recognized who it was, and then I remembered what he did for a living.

"Maryam, my Uncle Aharon," Ezra said stiffly. "He's decided to come around for a visit."

"It's good to see you again, Maryam," Aharon Brenner said. "You've grown into a beauty." He peered at me, examining my face, then sighed loudly, apparently not finding whatever he was looking for. The music ended in a screech as Ezra pulled the needle off the record.

"What do you want here, Aharon?"

"Ezra, please," I said. I was uncomfortable enough, and I didn't want to be in the middle of a family argument on top of it. I turned to Aharon Brenner. "We were just going to have some tea."

"That would be nice—thank you." He glanced significantly at Ezra as if to say: You see how to act? I felt like a traitor. I wondered what Riad would have to say if he could see me here, moving among them, moving this close. Aharon Brenner didn't have anything to say to me. We looked out of the glass doors to the patio. The area behind the apartment, up to a blocking row of tightly grown cypress trees, was walled and private, but beyond a small concrete apron it was desecrated by a neglected, weed-choked garden. My eyes fled it, as from a memory found to be false, rested on the portrait of Hannah Brenner, the shrine. Aharon Brenner followed my gaze, then smiled.

"Have you ever thought how fortunate we are, to have known our mythology in the flesh?"

"I think of it as a curse."

"Of course you do." He pointed at the painting. "So did Hannah."

"I know very little about her."

"Oh, we were all mad kids, mad with the idea of ourselves. You have to understand how mad it was; in Poland our lives centered on café arguments, and then suddenly, here we were, our discussions and disagreements translated to soil and light and flesh. Life was like a feverish

dream. Of course the reality of the situation eventually sunk
in. Ultimately, it didn't even allow our European dichoto-
mies to exist. Circumstances melded some of our old differences. Once, I remember, it was just after Hannah had gotten
pregnant with Ezra. Of all the times to be pregnant. She
wanted an abortion, naturally. This was during our period
of mutual outrage against the British. When my brother and
sister-in-law had had to come back from going back to the
soil. When our Haganah comrades had finally had enough.
You surely know some of the other times. You're a person
who knows our history, aren't you?"

Meaning the King David. I'd wondered how he'd insert
it into the conversation.

"But this time we were rescuing refugees. Lighting signal
fires on the beach, guiding in boatloads of pathetic wretches,
survivors from the camps. The British said drown, and we
were pulling the drowned from the sea, pulling them back
into life, as if we were young gods. Of course, some of them
did drown. One night we pulled the dead from the sea and
they stayed dead and Hannah pulled out a baby, a boy, naked, but with a number tattooed on his arm. God knows by
what miracle he'd been conceived, born, survived the camps.
She decided, at that moment, not to have the abortion. So
Ezra, you see, was a political gesture."

"So was I."

He looked from the portrait to me. "Only my nephew
refuses to admit it."

"I don't have the choice."

"No. Of course you don't. Tell me, how has Aida been?"

He'd given me his parable and was ready to move on.
But I wasn't sure what I was to get from it.

"Well, thank you."

"Does she ever mention those days?"

"Do you mean the King David? It was part of our family's mythology. As you are."

"I hope not as its devil—your parents were both stubborn people. I was sorry to hear of your father's death; he was always a man I felt we could come to some accommodation with, a man who could see beyond. Did he and Aida find what they were looking for when they went back to the West Bank? How did your . . . reassimilation work out?"

"Not as well as we thought it would."

"Ah? Why was that?"

"People didn't trust us because of the time we spent on the Jewish side. There was a dispute over the property also." I shrugged. "And it wasn't a life we were used to."

He smiled. "You were like diaspora Jews trying to return to the soil."

"I suppose you could make that comparison."

"But you wouldn't?"

"No."

Ezra came out of the kitchen, carrying a tray with a pot and three glasses on it. "Are you here to interrogate her?" he said.

Aharon Brenner smiled at me. "Is that how I sounded? I apologize, Maryam—I don't wish to make you uncomfortable. My questions are just the tics of an old policeman."

Ezra poured for us and sat down. He didn't look at his uncle. I touched my glass. It was very hot. Ezra picked up his glass and slowly tightened his hand around it, pressing it to his palm like a holy man gripping a burning coal. His uncle snorted and picked up his glass with no apparent feeling, the two men staring at each other, locked in some perverse contest of agony. I wondered what I was doing here, with these crazy Jews.

Ezra was silent on the way back, and I let it be. I wasn't sure what to make of the scene between him and his uncle, and I wasn't sure if I wanted to think about it too closely.

The village looked deserted when we drove through, and Aida wasn't home yet either. There was a note from her on the kitchen table, asking me to meet her at my uncle's house. Don't bring your friend, she'd written in Arabic. I helped Ezra bring the groceries inside. We packed them into the refrigerator and onto the pantry shelves. When we'd finished, Ezra went upstairs. He still hadn't spoken.

He came back down in a few minutes, wearing a T-shirt, cut-off jeans, and sneakers, his running clothes. He smiled at me.

"If you think you can keep up, you can come along."

At least his charm was intact. "Give me a few minutes to change," I said.

I went upstairs and put on shorts, a sleeveless T-shirt, and the Keds I'd worn all through school in the States. In

fact I hadn't dressed like this since being in the States, and I
hesitated before going back downstairs: it was crazy to go
outside here in this outfit. I looked at my image in the mirror: it leered at me like an arrogantly brazen tourist, a
stranger in my room. But a good-looking stranger. I
shrugged at the image and left the room.

"Come," I said.

"Are you sure?"

"Come."

I went out first, down the slope in front of the house,
moving along it diagonally to cut its steepness, following
the route I'd watched Ezra take every morning. He was close
behind me. At the bottom of the hill I ran across a flat space,
then up a hillock and across its crest. I began to stretch my
legs out, feeling a fool, hoping no one from the village would
see me. Jebel Halim was spread out behind me on its hill like
the white wake of my running; I turned and dipped off the
crest and into the deep gash of a wadi, and I was released,
cut from the village. The country closed around me. It was
as if we were alone in it. It was late afternoon, but the sun
was still strong, hot and pleasant on my shoulders and neck
and bare arms. Ezra came up next to me, breathing easily,
smiling. He'd taken his T-shirt off and reversed it, pulling
the neckhole down over his forehead and letting the shirt
hang over his shoulders like an Egyptian headdress. His chest
and shoulders were deeply tanned from the work he'd been
doing, his body neat and well-knit, with an hourglass of
wiry black hair swirling up from his belly to his chest. I
looked away. He ran by me with a kind of loose, snapping
grace and took the lead.

He picked up the pace. I was breathing hard. The air I
was drawing in seemed thickened with the heat, and my legs

started to feel heavy, full of sand. We were drawing parallel to the grove, on the other side of Jebel Halim. We'd made a large semicircle, halfway around the hill. Ezra turned and began scrambling up the side of the wadi. I stayed behind him. He ran faster. The bastard had no chivalry. We were going full speed now, racing the way we had when we were children, leaping rock to rock. I forgot the heaviness of my legs, my shortness of breath. We dipped down, then up the slope of Jebel Halim. I was light-headed with exhilaration. Ezra looked back at me over his shoulder, and suddenly I thought his face seemed stamped with panic, as if at my pursuit. But everything was blurred behind a veil of sweat. Near the top I gathered myself and put on another burst of speed. I drew up next to Ezra, and I must have been mistaken before, for he was grinning at me in approval. I looked away. Who'd asked him for it? We reached the top and threw ourselves down on the pine-fragrant ridge, laughing, listening to our voices ringing against the hills.

When I'd gotten my breath back, I said, "Wait here," and walked down to the house. I got a milk bottle filled with water and a bottle of the beer Ezra had bought and walked back. The air was still burning in my lungs. The water was so cold it made my throat ache. When Ezra banged the cap open on a rock, the beer foamed over his hand. He pressed the bottle to his forehead and closed his eyes. I waited for a compliment on my running. In vain.

"That was wonderful," I said. "What do we do now— scourge ourselves with thorns?"

He swigged at the beer, then smiled at me. "You've run before."

"In the States."

He nodded.

"Ezra, what was all that about? What did your uncle want?"

He held the bottle up in front of his face, squinting at the sun. An amoeba shape of gold light flowed over his skin.

"Maybe all our uncles have to die in the wilderness—before we can build the promised land." He lowered the bottle. "Or maybe that's just more poetry."

It was growing dark, the shadows pooling around the wrecked car below and lengthening toward us in stretching fingers. Over in Jerusalem rows of lights were blinking on, like the lights of a ship passing at sea. Ezra put his hand on the back of my hair, pressing it down, then smoothing it. A shudder passed through me. He put his other arm around me, leaning in, his breath warm on my face. There was an inevitability about his movements, an inexorable ritual of possession that made me feel trapped. I put my hand on his chest, feeling his skin and hair warm against my palm. I pushed him away anyway.

"Why?" he asked.

"Nothing has changed since the last time we were on this ridge. We still haven't stepped outside of the atmosphere."

He took his arm from my shoulder and nodded, looking off into the darkness, at the scattered clusters of lights in it.

"No," he said. "Nothing has changed. Look, I'm sorry."

"There's no need . . ."

Come, let's go back to the house. The seminar is over."

"Ezra, please."

"I won't touch you. Come."

In the house, I went upstairs and changed. He was standing in the living room when I came down.

"I'll be back in a little while. I have to meet Aida."

"Maybe I'd better leave."

"Don't be silly. Stay," I said, the word slipping out of my mouth like a traitor. Stay bomber. Stay terror. Don't go. Perhaps I'll bring you my own confessions one day; we'll achieve symmetry.

"I don't want you to leave like this," I said. "Stay at least for tonight."

He shrugged. "Why not."

I wondered if he'd be there when I got back. After I'd closed the door I wanted to run back inside to him. To keep running in circles. I walked to my uncle's house instead.

All the lights were on upstairs, and I heard the sounds of an argument coming from the windows. Individual words drifted out to me, protest, oppression, strike back—the weights that kept me from drifting out into space. I went in the front door. The living room was dark. As I started for the stairs, Riad stepped out in front of me. Like an angry husband. He'd want to know where I'd been, who I'd seen, and I'd have to lie, hide the lover who hadn't touched me from the husband who hadn't touched me.

"Stay here for a moment, Maryam. Let's talk."

He led me back to the living room and switched on a lamp. We sat down. I could still feel the wetness of Ezra's skin on my palm: I closed my hand around it, over a secret. The voices upstairs grew louder.

"What are they arguing about?"

"How to respond to a crime. Your mother, as always, is the voice of moderation," he said with disgust.

"What crime?"

"You can get the details when you go up. But I need

to speak to you now."

His face was half in shadow. The half that I could see smiled at me.

"What do you think you're doing?" he asked. "With that Jew?"

"What do you mean?"

He laughed. "Do you think there's anything you do here that's not seen? Having him in your house. Naked in the hills with him."

"We weren't naked. We were running."

"Running?" His laugh grew incredulous. "Wonderful. Running. Your mother's position here is precarious enough. Maryam, there's a man upstairs, above our heads now, who slit his own daughter's throat as if she were a sheep because she was caught sleeping with a Christian. Everyone in the village knows what he did, but they all pretend to believe him when he says his daughter is in Beirut."

"My mother converted—"

Riad held up his hand. "That girl's lover had to run away from the country—and he's an Arab. How do you think people will feel about what you're doing?"

"I've done nothing."

"What actually happened isn't important, do you understand? What's important is how you're perceived."

"Riad, you wanted me to meet him, see him again."

"To meet him. To be introduced to Breira. Not to lose the respect of your own people. Why do you think your mother is upstairs, allowed to speak in our council? Because of your father's name. It's your name too."

"What do you want from me?"

He was silent for a moment. Then he said, "Come to us. Now."

"I need more time."

"There is no more time."

"Aida will never let me go—you know how she feels," I said hopelessly.

"I'm confident that you'll find a way."

I woke to the sound of blows thudding over my head. For a few seconds I wasn't sure if they weren't coming from inside my skull: after Maryam had left me at the house the night before, I'd finished most of a bottle of commemorative slivovitz.

I called Maryam's name, then Aida's. There was no answer. I'd been alone in the house before I'd fallen asleep. The two of them hadn't gotten back from wherever it was they'd had to go.

Another series of blows hit fitfully on the roof.

I stuck my head out the window. A rock hit the wall below me. A small figure darted around to the side of the house. I heard a flurry of laughter. Three more figures ran toward the house. Each flung a stone and ran away. They were kids, two boys and a girl, maybe nine or ten years old. They ran off a few meters, stopped, and looked back at me, their bodies poised between flight and attack.

I went through the house, checking room to room. Neither of their beds looked slept in. From Maryam's window I could see a crowd of children gathering. They were picking up stones and looking up at me, their faces old with hate: what they were doing had taken away their childhood and transformed them into a race of tough, malevolent dwarfs. A girl in a school uniform, blue dress with trousers beneath it, cupped her hands and began screaming at me in a shrill, accusatory voice.

I leaned outside so that I could see to the village. Knots of people were forming and coming apart on the main street. A few more stones hit around me. I was making the house into a target by being here. For that matter, my being here had probably already made Maryam and Aida into the targets of the mob.

The thought pushed me downstairs. I hesitated for a second, then burst open the front door and came out running. I had to hope for surprise. The children did stop for a few seconds, then began closing in on me. I pulled open the front door of the Land-Rover and jumped in, releasing the brake and starting the engine on the roll. Stones bounced off the roof and hood. There was a loud crash. I glanced in the mirror and saw that the rear window had been starred. I was bouncing wildly down the path to the village. Too fast. I downshifted and slowed.

The path widened into the village street. An angry face suddenly loomed in front of the windshield and a spatulate hand slapped the glass in front of my face. I stamped on the brake and the man slid off the hood. He had a gaunt, pocked face and splayed teeth and was wearing a knit ski cap with a pom-pom on it that made him look at once comical and deadly. He began pounding on the hood with his fist. More faces were crowding the windows. Their mouths opened and closed, the movement somehow disconnected from the screaming all around me: an out of sync movie. Fists beat insistently on the roof. I turned the motor off, pocketed the keys, and pushed my door open. There was a shriek and a general rise in the level of the noise. I wasn't sure what I was going to do, but anything seemed better than being trapped inside.

Maybe not. Hands grabbed me roughly, bodies pressed in on me. The man in the ski cap was screaming in my face, his spittle spraying me. He began shoving me backward, pushing open palmed at my chest, like a schoolboy trying to provoke a fight. I kept my hands at my sides. There was a surge in the crowd, and several young men carrying palm fronds broke through the front rank. They began swishing the sharp-edged leaves in front of my face. When I didn't react they started to smack them against my chest and shoulders. The mob started to chant, *"Yahud, Yahud, Yahud."* Jew. I was going to die in a pogrom, some distant, amused spectator in my head said to me.

The crowd had closed around me like a trap. The pitch of sound rose impossibly. The man in the ski cap took a frond from one of the young men and whipped it across my face, once, twice. He didn't curse at me now, just stared, his eyes cold and appraising. He pushed the tip of the frond at my mouth and eyes, as if searching for a breaking point. I grabbed the tip and broke it off. I could feel the current of excitement in the crowd get stronger, as if I were one of them. I was beyond being afraid or even feeling pain. It was something that had happened to me before, in combat, and I was dimly grateful it was happening now. Someone shoved me, and I fell back hard into the wall of a house.

A very small old woman with a broad, strong face suddenly appeared in front of me. She was waving her arms at
the mob and screaming in a high, pecking voice. The men
in the front rank winced at her words and began backing
off, exchanging the half-ashamed, half-proud looks men give
each other when they are scolded by their own strong old
women. The palm fronds dangled from their hands like toys
they'd been told not to play with.

A tall, thin man in a dark pin-striped suit broke roughly
through the crowd. He had a craggy, handsome face, with
a black crow's wing of hair brushed across his forehead. I
recognized the face: it had stared out of one of the niches at
the Halims' house: Maryam's uncle, the village mukhtar.
Maryam and Aida came pushing through behind him. Both
of them looked painfully embarrassed, as if they were
ashamed of the riot as a breach of hospitality.

"He's a friend," Maryam said, then added, "You bas-
tards." In Hebrew.

"Don't," I said. "You might provoke them."

She looked at me wildly and laughed. The mukhtar said
something sharply to her that I couldn't hear. He began to
push me toward the Land-Rover.

I opened the driver's door and the passenger door behind
it. For a minute neither Aida nor Maryam moved. The villagers were slowly forming another circle, around the car. I
could feel the pushing weight of them. A sense of strong
water being held back by a very thin dam. Aida spat on the
ground, her face pale with anger. I grabbed Maryam by the
shoulders and pushed her into the backseat. When I touched
her there was a hiss of drawn breaths. A flash of rage jumped
across the mukhtar's face and onto Aida's. Then she nodded
tightly and climbed into the car, next to Maryam. I got be-

hind the wheel and closed the door. Triumphant, mocking
yells broke from some of the villagers, as though a victory
had been won.

I started the car and performed an agonizingly slow, broken U-turn. People moved from my path with mocking
lethargy. I fought the urge to run them down.

Inside, we sat around the kitchen table, the embarrassment
of survivors lying between us.

"Thank you for rescuing me from my rescue," I said
finally.

"Is *that* what it was?" Maryam asked.

"That was the idea."

"My God," Aida said.

"Are you both all right?"

"Were you mad, Ezra?" Aida stared at me. "Why did you
do it?"

"I thought I was the cause of the riot—that they were
after you about me."

She kept staring at me.

"What the hell happened?" I asked. I felt a rise of annoyance. At their failure to praise my noble stupidity, I suppose.
Aida turned away. Suddenly neither of them would look
at me.

"What happened?" I repeated.

"There was a meeting last night, all night, in the mukhtar's house," Aida said. "I tried to get the people in it to be
reasonable. I didn't succeed."

I tried to hold on to my patience. "Reasonable about
what? Was the meeting about me being here?"

Maryam blinked at me and shook her head, as if coming
awake. "No. A boy was shot yesterday, in Hebron. He threw

a stone at a settler's car and the settler shot him. There were riots yesterday and two schoolgirls were shot and killed by some other West Bank Jewish cowboy. That was what the meeting was about, Ezra. Not about you. About courses of action. About what to do.''

Her voice was strident, the rhythms of the arguments she must have been involved in the night before still echoing in it. The wail of a siren came through the window, and I saw Aida shudder. I felt sick at the speed with which things could fall apart.

"I'd better go," I said. "Even if it wasn't about me. There were some kids stoning the house before, and I just made my presence very obvious, with that little drive. I'll just bring more trouble to you."

"For your own safety too," Aida agreed quickly. "And not that we're not grateful."

Maryam stared at me, her eyes bright with intensity.

"I'm going with you," she said with surprise, as if it were something she'd just realized.

Aida turned slowly to her, her face red.

"You're not going anywhere. Not now."

I hadn't taken my eyes off Maryam since she'd spoken. "If not now, when?" I said.

Aida laughed harshly. "How biblical you Jews always manage to get when you want to take something."

Maryam stood up, her eyes opaqued, unfocused with anger. Aida looked at her for a moment, then shrugged.

"If you go," she said, "don't come back."

Maryam walked out of the room. I heard her go upstairs. Aida kept her eyes locked to mine. She shook her head in wonder, as if we were both sharing her daughter's unreasonableness. I heard Maryam come back down. The front door slammed.

I went after her.

When I caught up, she was standing by the big tree, her face pale against the burn mark. She had a large handbag on her shoulder. She was looking around the grove as if memorizing a picture of it to take into exile. As if there were going to be a wedding there after all.

"Not here," I heard myself say.

We walked to the Land-Rover. I could see down to the main street of the village. It looked suddenly deserted. The house, behind us, was closed and dark, as if Aida were already mourning me. I didn't look back at it as we drove away. The doors and windows of the houses were closed tight and the metal shutters pulled down in front of the shops. Closed to me. There were rocks scattered everywhere and twists of oily smoke turning and thinning in the air, their points of origin hidden behind the roofs.

A jeep suddenly pulled in front of us. It had a machine gun mounted on its crossbar. A helmeted soldier pointed the gun at me. For my sins. Two other soldiers jumped out and came to each side of the Land-Rover. Ezra rolled down the window. The soldier on my side yanked open the door and pointed his Uzi at me.

"Identification, please," the soldier on Ezra's side said. Ezra slowly took out his wallet, then patted my arm. "It's OK, just take out your card." I gave it to him, and he handed the two cards out through the window. The soldier studied Ezra's ID.

"What the hell are you doing here?"

"Visiting friends."

The soldier looked at my card. A sneer formed on his face. "Check under the seats," he said to the other man. The second soldier poked under my seat, then under the passenger seat and the tarp in the back.

"In order," he said.

The first soldier handed the cards back to Ezra.

"Take your *friend* and get out of here. This is no place for you."

We drove out of the village, past a border of smoking tires.

"Where are we going?" I asked.

"My house. If that's all right with you. I haven't really thought about it."

"I have. I know a place."

He took his eyes off the road for a second and looked at me, his face registering the idea that I'd thought about it. I told him where to drive.

We went down from Jerusalem. I watched the hills change, their rock-bony slopes suddenly covered, hidden by the pine forests planted over the last twenty-five years like a mantle thrown over a brazen nudity. Villages on the crests threw the light off the flat sides of their houses in frantic signals to me. Stop. Past Abu Ghosh. Past the rusted hulls of armored cars lying by the side of the road, laced with shadows and petaled with the remains of the wreaths people had left on them. The trees began to thin out. We were suddenly in the green, open, undulating country of the coastal plain. I felt as if a clamp had been loosened from my forehead. The landscape seemed limitless. Plains and mountains, the variety of geography giving the small land illusions of vastness. Or the borders I knew about putting an illusion of constriction and limit on a vast land, on Asia. I felt a need to fill myself with distance. The glitter of an irrigation pipe raced the car. We drove through Ramle, once an Arab town, and rows of young men squatted like crows on the iron railings along the sidewalk and stared at me. We passed the airport. When we were outside Tel Aviv, Ezra stopped for gas, and we both used the rest room.

"Go north," I said, when he came out.

Past Haifa the road stayed close to the sea. I watched it flinging lace froth up on the sand, drawing the beach back to itself, claiming it with that light, persistent weight. Past Akko I saw the white cliffs of Rosh Hanikra marking the Lebanese border. We were running out of country. The sign marking the national park at Achziv was on the right side of the road, with an arrow pointing back to the other side. "There," I said, and Ezra turned.

We parked the Land-Rover and walked down over neatly clipped lawns spaced evenly with tall palm trees to the ruins. After them was a sudden cliff going down to a small, rocky beach. It was a workday, and the place was deserted. There were the weaving shades and turquoises and azures of the water and the beach and the cliff and the ruins and the park and after it the flat farm country of the Jezreel and then the mountains, the rest of the world, all the distance I wanted. We walked down to the beach on steps cut into the face of the cliff. The rocky crescent was enclosed on its north and south sides by rows of barbed wire. Beyond the wire on the southern side was a long stretch of white sand beach dotted with thatched huts, like an abandoned Polynesian village. It was the site of what was to be an international vacation club, its construction delayed by labor problems. It was as devoid of people as Riad had said it would be.

Ezra placed a piece of driftwood over the wire and we stepped across. It was nearly dark. We entered the first hut we came to. And stood inside, neither of us speaking or looking at the other.

"Wait," Ezra said. He pulled his shirt out from his chest and sniffed himself. "I stink." He went back out.

"Where are you going?"

I followed him to the beach. He walked toward the water, pulling his shirt over his head and throwing it on the sand. At the edge of the sea he stripped off his clothes and stood naked, beautiful, in silver light. He looked at me over his shoulder, then laughed and plunged in.

I stared at the flat sheets of dying sunlight reflecting off the water. Ezra's head suddenly appeared, shattering the light into pieces. He yelled and splashed, slapping his chest and shoulders. He hadn't said that I stank. But perhaps he was just being polite. Wondering at myself, looking at myself with wonder, I took off my clothing, down to my gooseflesh, and ran into the water.

Ice, then fire. My skin was burned clean. Then Ezra was next to me, barrel-rolling, yelling. Laughter shook us, the way it had a century before, running in the hills. I felt mad with freedom. He put his arms around me and kissed me, my lips, my throat, my breasts, lifting me from the water.

On the sand, he said, his voice catching in his throat, "I feel like we're kids again. Playing 'show me.'"

"You've grown," I said, and felt myself blushing in the sudden darkness. He laughed and we gathered our clothes, drying with them as we walked to the hut. Inside was a pile of collapsed cots. We set up two of them and pushed them together. Listening to the waves breaking outside was like being in the cabin of a ship at sea. I felt with a shock the smoothness of our skin touching, an uninterrupted caress, and we came together with the gentleness of lovers who already knew all of each other's secrets.

He slept finally, his back to me. For a long time I stared, transfixed, at the breathing solidity of him lying next to me, the lines of his back and hips. He was outlined by moon- and sea-light filtering through the thatch, his flesh known and there but somehow still ephemeral. I started to drift off, but I fought myself awake, focusing on a need to stay as long as I could outside the atmosphere. "Ezra," I whispered, trying to shake away the galloping panic I felt. He turned around to me, then lay on his side, looking at me, his eyes shining.

"I thought I'd wake up and you wouldn't be here," he said.

"I'm here."

"Are you all right?"

"Yes," I said, my last lie of the day.

When I woke up the cot next to mine was empty, as if my uneasy dreams had taken a solid shape. The sunlight was coming in through the weave of the thatch, making spots of money on the canvas and on my skin. I lay still for a while, listening to the waves hitting the beach. She'd probably gone for a walk or a swim. I was grateful for the time alone. The world had changed again in a day and a night, and I needed time to think about the shift. About what was going to happen next. Maybe she just needed to be alone also. I wondered what it was either one of us could solve. Israelis of different religions sometimes went to Cyprus to get married. But I wasn't sure if that was what she wanted or what I wanted and even the reasonable phrase I'd created, Israelis of different religions, was insane.

I got out of the cot and went to the door of the hut. The beach was empty. I walked down to the water. A thin film of sea washed the pebbles near my feet. For a moment they gleamed, brilliant as jewels, and then the water retreated and their distinction faded. There were pottery shards and broken soda bottles mixed in with them. I waded out and dove in.

The sea was warm and textured on my skin. I narrowed my field of vision to just my hands falling into the water in front of me, pulling it to me, and tried to stop thinking. So where do you go now? I thought. I swam back. When I got out of the water the breeze cooled the wetness on my back. I went to the hut, dried off with my shirt, and got dressed.

I walked down the beach, crossed back over the wire, and went up through the ruins. On top of the cliff was a private museum run by the famous recluse who lived at Achziv. A wooden, prowlike roof was jammed down haphazardly, buckled, over a stone first floor, the boards loose and flapping, bleached by the sun. The whole structure hung off to one side, like an architect's bad joke. I knocked at the door. A blond woman dressed in dungaree shorts and a halter answered. I asked if a woman had come inside. She nodded doubtfully, looking at me, and I realized how I must appear to her, stubble-bearded and crusted with salt, my clothes damp and wrinkled: the image of a castaway.

"There's a three-lira admission charge," she said.

I paid and went inside. It was cool and dark, so different from outside that I had the sensation of being swallowed. A slim, dark man in a red-checked, short-sleeved shirt and neatly pressed white linen trousers passed me, going out as if the museum had felt compelled to send a more suitable replacement into the world. His eyes met mine for a second, then they flitted away. On the walls and floors of the corridor and in the rooms off it were a mixture of artifacts, all from Achziv: Philistine pottery, the rusted compass and wheel of a wrecked British sloop, Roman coins, stones bearing the graffiti of Crusaders, the arched struts of wooden boats framing doorways. Dozens of small clay fertility goddesses had been hung by cords from the ceiling; they clinked together as the breeze came through the chinks in the large boards that blocked the windows. The people who ran the museum seemed to live among the exhibits: there was furniture—wooden dressers, beds, and cots scattered through the artifacts like illustrations of the modern world. A Roman pillar served as nightstand to one bed, an alarm clock and lamp sat on it. I began going from one room to another. Maryam was in the fourth, sitting on an old brass bed, surrounded by artifacts. She looked up at me dully.

"I'm sorry," she said.

I sat down next to her. "It's OK—I just got worried."

She shook her head. "I wasn't coming back."

An echo of the feeling I'd had when I woke up and found her cot empty passed sharply through me: my bad dreams made solid, put into words.

"Where are you going?"

She didn't answer for a minute. I thought of the man I'd passed on the way in, then I thought about the white cliffs of Rosh Hanikra and the enemy country beyond them.

"You know where I'm going," she said.

"When did you choose?" I asked.

She stared at me. "After the meeting yesterday. A year ago. The day I was born. What's the difference?"

"I wanted to know if that's the only reason we're here. But you're right, it doesn't make any difference."

She trailed her finger along the surface of the mattress.

"It's not that simple," she said. "I told myself it was only that also. But it was more. I wanted to give you something, to leave myself with something."

"And now all your debts are clear. You owe nothing. And you can still go to them clean—nothing we did touched you. You can still carry a certificate of virginity."

"Please, Ezra, that isn't fair. What else is there to do?"

"We could go to Cyprus. Someplace. Any place."

"There is no place."

"I just named one. I'll leave this crazy museum of a country and go there with you."

"I don't have a country to leave for you. I have to get one first. Can you understand that?"

"It's just more fucking poetry," I said.

PART TWO

. . . . EZRA

Beit Harim edged out of my memory below the high ridge
where I stopped: white houses with red tile roofs and tree-
shaded lawns capping a bare brown hill, all of it surrounded
by a barbed-wire perimeter and spider-legged watchtowers.
The kibbutz fields were laid out in green-and-yellow carpet
squares around the base of the hill; their flatness ended at the
wide dirt road and the fence that marked the northern border.

I drove down to the kibbutz. The graveled road stopped
at the office, and I parked next to it. When I walked inside,
I thought I saw a brief look of distress cross Amnon Sapir's face, a host annoyed at the acceptance of an invita-
tion extended only out of politeness. But he smiled at me
warmly.

"Ezra! What brings you?"

"I was on vacation, near Rosh Hanikra . . ." I said.

I hadn't been ready to go back to Jerusalem. When I'd
left Achziv, the kibbutz, not far away, had hung in my mind,
an encysted image from my childhood, protected by an in-

sularity so strong it seemed it could deny the inevitable disappointments of time.

"And so you decided to pay a call," Amnon said, with satisfaction. "Good. Come on, we'll get something to eat, some coffee. Yardena will be delighted to see you but angry she wasn't here when you came—she's at the clinic in Kfar Maya'an today. Come, let's put something into your stomach."

"I've already eaten."

"Some coffee then. Come on, Ezra, I need an excuse to get out of my office."

We walked to the dining hall. It had been about six years since I'd been to the kibbutz, though when I was a child my father would bring me every summer. The revolving lawn sprinklers still made their tap-hiss, tap-hiss sound. Bomb shelters stuck up here and there like blunted shark fins swimming in the smooth expanse of grass. Their sides were painted with brightly colored murals of doves, olive branches, and ban-the-bomb symbols, amulets against the very danger they signaled. Lines of red and yellow carnations and tulips gridded the lawn; they marked the edges of trenches that were inner-faced with sheets of corrugated tin and reinforced by upside-down U-joints. The sprinklers were the same, but neither the shelters nor the trenches had been here the last time I'd visited. Before the last war, this had been a mostly friendly border, from the time my mother and father and fifteen other earnest Russian and Polish boys and girls had come to the hill and spread their mattresses out under the stars on the first night of the kibbutz. The watchtowers and shelters had been built when shelling started from Lebanon, and the barbed wire strung a little later, after four terrorists had crossed the border one night, hitched a ride with a young couple from the settlement, cut their throats, and driven the jeep into the kibbutz. They'd been shot down by Amnon, who'd caught them attaching explosives to the wall of a house.

A sign on the side of the dining hall named the building after my father. I formed a shadow under it into a picture of Maryam crouched by the dining-room wall, ready to turn love into a weapon, ready, as I'd been, to obliterate memory. We went inside. Amnon took two cups from a tray on the serving table, filled them with coffee from the large aluminum percolator. We sat at a table. The hall was empty except for a woman mopping the floor, her sandals flapping against the stone floor.

"Can you stay for a while?" Amnon asked.

"I'd like to."

"Good. You can stay with Yardena and me—we'll fix up my study."

"I don't want to put you out."

"Nonsense."

"Look, if you have room in the volunteer quarters . . . "

He peered at me, wrinkling his forehead, then nodded. "Room we have, plenty; since the shelling we don't take foreigners. OK, sure. I won't ask questions. You want to come to a commune to be a recluse, *bavakasha*, please, be my guest. No questions. No pressure. Are you all right?"

"I just need more vacation."

"You know how I felt about your father—he should have never left us. Do you understand? Stay as long as you want, stay forever, you get me, Ezra? Listen, how's your Uncle Aharon? Does he still regard us as a cloistered refuge for left-wing relics? I'm not surprised. Sometimes I think he's right. Never mind, that's just clever talk. Don't take me seriously. There's a strange duck, your uncle. All the women we tried to set him up with. Nothing. No interest. Your father used to say that Aharon felt he personally impregnated history to give birth to the State. What could replace such a sensation? You understand, Amos would say that. I wouldn't presume."

He took a crumpled pack of Nadivs out of his shirt and offered me one. When I shook my head, he tapped out one for himself and lit it.

"I'll be glad to work while I'm here," I said.

"Glad to work? Did you think you had a choice?" *You work only if you want to. If you want to eat.* Amnon peered at me, then looked at his cigarette with disgust and ground it out in the cup. "I'll show you your luxurious quarters."

I followed him across the trench-canaled lawn to a low, ramshackle building with fly-speckled screen doors rattling along its front—one of the original structures of the kibbutz. My father and mother might have even lived here. A stand made from two stacked egg crates was in front of one door and, on top of it, a tin bowl half-filled with scummy water. Amnon squinted at the water with distaste.

"Look—are you sure you don't want to stay with Yardena and me?"

"I'll be all right here."

"You'll be alone. As I said, normally we'd have volunteers . . ."

"Has the shelling been bad?"

"Not too bad, here; our only casualties had feathers. We took a Katuysha in the chicken house—for a week we ate chicken and shit shrapnel. Listen, I'll assign you to cotton, with Ahia, tomorrow. Then up to the cattle station—I can use someone who knows the country up there. Is that all right?"

"Whatever you say."

Amnon opened the door. The room was boxlike and stifling hot, furnished with a cot and a doorless plywood closet. The Brenner memorial room. A cell.

"This will be fine," I said.

I began work well before dawn the next day, weeding with a tractor, then shifting around grids of aluminum irrigation pipes, getting in two hours of work before the real heat of the day started. When it got close to sunrise, colors began to sneak into the sky and earth, the bulked shape of the mountains leaking faint streaks of gray and pink, then blazing as if ignited into incandescent greens and yellows. As soon as the sun rose it was very hot, and Ahia and I stopped for breakfast. We sat against the wheels of the big Massey-Ferguson 450 tractors, two heavy shields of metal bolted on each side of the drivers' seats for protection against snipers, and we ate halvah and hard-boiled eggs and drank the thick as mud kibbutz coffee Ahia had brought in his thermos. He was a heavy-shouldered, blunt-faced man in his fifties, who as long as I knew him was touched by silence, his communication with the world channeled into the effortless, delicate grace and respect with which he treated tools and objects. When I'd worked here as a teenager, I liked to ruffle his calm by deliberately being imprecise about his tools: "Hand me a wrench, will you, Ahia?" "That's an eleven-sixteenth, Ezra— can't you say that? An eleven-sixteenth."

Mount Hermon's ice white peak floated disembodied over the fields in the hard blue sky to the northeast, like a mirage carried down from some far Caucasian range, so beautiful it made something inside me drop. The flanks of the Lebanese mountains in front of us were dotted with villages, their white houses glittering like specks of mica in the sun. I could see the Good Fence, the border, twisting serpentine over the hills. For a moment I entertained the idea of Maryam, on the other side, looking over at me.

There was a crescendoing whistle. The ground about thirty meters from me boiled up in a dirty cloud. The blast stung my cheeks and set my ears ringing. I stood perfectly still—there was no place to hide in the flat cotton field anyway. Ahia brushed off his hands against his trousers and walked over to me, his eyes roaming over the tractors, checking for damage.

"Katuysha," he said, as if he were naming locusts or hail.

He pointed. A few seconds later I spotted several bright winks of fire on the far slopes, signals from the enemy country where she had gone.

This morning I found that the furniture in the living room had been rearranged while I slept, everything pushed to the sides of the room, with only two rattan chairs left facing each other in the middle of the tile grid of the floor, like surviving chess pieces. I sat in one of the chairs.

I sit in the chair now, waiting. Writing a letter to you in my head. Running the last weeks through my mind as if I can let you share my journey, bring you with me. When I stepped away from Achziv, I stepped into a shaft that kept opening under me and then I was here. No, you're right, it wasn't that simple, or rather, it's simple only in hindsight. I'd assumed I'd be taken over the border at Rosh Hanikra, for example, but it was only a ruse, Riad said, not to worry, there'd be no crawling under wires, no dramatics. Instead there was merely a little drive in the family car to the airport and a packed Samsonite and an airline ticket and the passport I'd already given Riad. When did you choose? you asked me. But there was no exact moment, that was the shaft: I simply allowed myself to step into it and fall, a motion over which I had no control.

No dramatics either, as promised. My ticket was for Athens via Farmagusta, a common route for Israeli-Arabs who wanted to meet relatives from the Arab countries on neutral ground. I'd made the same trip, in fact, which was, I suppose, why they chose the route for me. They even booked me on El Al, perhaps as a joke. I hope so. Somehow it's comforting to think of the people I'm with now as having a sense of humor. Admittedly, it wasn't that funny at the time. The customs agent, a plump, red-haired woman, had glanced at my name and proclaimed with icy sweetness: "How *wise.* The national airline *is* the safest against terrorist attacks." And until the airplane was actually off the ground, I'd waited for the grip of a hand on my shoulder, dragging me back.

We landed in Cyprus, the country you proposed as a haven. Love's happy kingdom, torn by its own civil war. A man in a white linen suit took my Israeli passport, handed me a Lebanese passport, and escorted me to the Middle Eastern Airlines counter without a word. Ten minutes later I was on a plane again. A spaceship. Because then I was in Beirut. Just like that. Just as if I'd say: And then I was on Mars.

A Martian met me, a tall woman, her eyes outlined heavily with kohl. She embraced me warmly, a younger sister come home, kissed me on both cheeks, and then, as if her repertoire of human responses had been exhausted, lapsed into a silence from which she never recovered. In silence she took me to her car, in silence she drove me to this apartment building and deposited me in a flat on the tenth floor.

"Wait," she said, as she left.

I waited. A succession of visitors, new faces every day, came in, prepared my meals, inquired politely about my health—"I have *leprosy,*" I said—smiled sympathetically, and left. The windows in the flat had metal blinds, which were kept almost completely shut, allowing only thin bars of sunlight to stripe the rugless, endless white of the tile floor. During the day I peered through the blinds at the first Arab capital I'd ever seen, at the shoppers thronging below my window, as much the self-consciously amazed tourist as an American Jew visiting Israel, astonished at the Jewish country, at Jewish stevedores and policemen and criminals. At night the street was deserted and there was a constant crackle of gunfire, punctuated by the exclamation marks of explosions. From the radios my visitors would sometimes bring with them, I heard broadcasts telling with shrill nervousness of rumors about an impending Israeli invasion, and the gunfire at night seemed to respond frantically, as if there were an anxiousness in the city to get in some quota of internecine killing before it was too late. Before I'd see you through the bars of my window, see you jump from your half-track, dusty and tanned and handsome and running up the stairs to me, an Uzi gripped tightly in your hands, unsure of the welcome you'd get as I'm unsure of the welcome I'd give.

I was taken out of this place only once, bundled down to the front of the building at dawn and told to stand with three stony-faced young men. Blinking at the sunlight like a released prisoner, I did as instructed. As soon as I'd inserted myself in the center of the group, the young men's hard faces melted into beaming smiles; we were all extras playing a part again, and they draped their arms around one another's necks and my own, then froze as an old box Leica was unveiled in front of us and a series of pictures taken. *"Giveneh,"* I said in Hebrew, somewhat dizzily. "Cheese."

When we were finished, they brought me upstairs again. "Wait," they said.

. . . . .EZRA

The grass was gilded by the first light, and Mount Hermon's gleaming snow face hung impossibly close, like a nosy god. I worked my way over the low stone walls that gridded the area and shaped the work—it was impossible to use horses or jeeps to herd the cattle. The sun pressed down pleasantly on me. The shapes of the cattle moved ahead of me on the plain, connected to me invisibly by the detached, extended hand that was the dog. At night the cattle would wander toward the Syrian border, and every day we'd have to drive them back to the west, a man and dog team dropped off by jeep every few kilometers and converging, the cattle before us, on a grove of trees that served as a reference point. The dogs, who did most of the work, were intelligent German shepherds; the men would walk behind them carrying rifles, as if we were only there to guard them, which, essentially, we were.

My dog and I were dropped off last, at the northern border of the grazing area. It took me an hour to catch up with the first group of strays. They faced me in a circle, the bunched muscles under their sleeked coats twitching as if galvanized. My dog ran around their circle, nipping them in, barking frantically, darting under and biting the bellies of the bolder cows who were trying to break away. I ran after him, waving and yelling, the dog glancing at me worriedly, as if doubting I was taking this task, his life's work, seriously enough.

As soon as he had the cows trotting in the right direction, I slowed down. I was nearly at the edge of the plateau, where it dropped off into a deep valley, a fold in the plateau. A vertical wall rose up on the other side of the valley, sheened with yellow grass. The valley floor was patched with trees, their spreads of leaves deep green against the burned yellow, and a kilometer or so ahead the valley narrowed and was closed by a plug of black cliff that was bisected by the twisting, silver ribbon of a waterfall. The beauty was shocking when I thought about what I'd seen the last time I was on the Golan, but all of that was cleaned off and hidden and I had a sense of the country seen by my mother and father, its distances trembling with promise, with the illusion of emptiness.

The dog suddenly dashed off into a bank of high grass, barking after some hidden strays. I unslung the old bolt-action Czech rifle I was carrying and sat down on an outcrop of black volcanic rock to wait for him. A blue teakettle sat near me on another rock, abandoned, holding a suggestion of flight and loneliness. The village it had probably come from, abandoned also, stared down with windows like black, sightless eyes from a nearby rise.

From where I was sitting I could suddenly see that there were pieces of jagged, rusted metal scattered all through the riffling grass, revealed in parting glimpses by the wind. I let my eyes follow a trail that led to the pocked hull of a destroyed Syrian tank, peeking out of the tall grass like a half-buried memory. I looked away, back down to the refuge of the valley. Below me, a herd of boar broke suddenly from the trees and ran silently across the valley floor—the black border of water after a wave has broken and it moves smoothly and swiftly over the sand. I thought I heard the echoing crack of a shot, tinny and distant.

I forced myself to look back at the tank. I hadn't been up here since the war, and I thought about how easy the country made it to cross back into the killing ground. It was only a short drive away, and even, in Jerusalem, a short walk; always there, waiting, as my parents' vision had been, under the illusion of beauty. Maryam's father had written a poem that started: "The border is the line of a wound." Unsubtle, didactic, she'd call it, and then she'd cross the line and go make her own memories. The line we'd held would be farther to the east of here: if I climbed the hillock the village was on I'd probably be able to see it. When we'd taken over the position the bodies in front of us had still been locked with the enemy dead, literally and physically the border of the country. The border as flesh, as a hard seam of wound; it existed under the illusion of myself, the illusion of freedom, as it existed in Maryam. We hadn't crossed it but carried it with us to the false refuge of Achziv and she with her to the false refuge of Lebanon, and now I'd come back to the bucolic prettiness and red roofs and the ideal green fields of my childhood, the pretty island my parents had seeded and nourished on a sea of madness. I closed my eyes, and when I opened them I could see the metal of war, solidly real and unsubtle and scattered among the rocks and grass.

I ate dinner at Amnon and Yardena's table near the serving line, where the older members of the kibbutz gravitated. Ahia sat silently on my right, listening to the Israeli news broadcast about the damage the Katuyshas had done in the attacks this week, and then switching to a Lebanese station and shrill reports of innocent women and children buried in the rubble of the Israeli counterattacks. His large hand on the table opened and closed helplessly, as if it needed something to turn or twist. I told Amnon I'd been there long enough, and asked if there'd be any trouble covering my work load if I left. A look of pain crossed his face, but he said there'd be no problem, none at all, and come again, anytime, you belong here.

I left for Jerusalem late the next morning. When I arrived it was Saturday night and the streets were crowded. Gauntlets of teenagers perched atop the guardrails along the sidewalks, calling to one another, chewing sunflower seeds and spitting the hulls into slimy heaps in the gutters. The squares of light cast by the shop windows momentarily froze passing couples into photographs: dark-haired girls in army shirts, their hands resting lightly on the shoulders of tall, awkward boys, the fragility of their youth caught and emphasized for an instant. When I walked into the Gallery, everyone greeted me effusively, as if I'd been gone for years. The narrow walls of the café squeezed around me.

I ordered a bottle of cognac. I was nearly at the bottom of it when Deddy and Yael came into the café. Deddy's face lit up when he saw me; then a frown crossed it, a register of concern.

"What's happening with you?" he asked. "We haven't seen you around."

I pushed a chair out with my foot, than another. "Sit."

"Where have you been?—we've missed you. There's a lot going on; we're thinking of running a list for Knesset."

I felt a rise of annoyance at Deddy. I was angry at my journey's ending, at it coming to rest here. Rabbi Gur. Rabbi Gur and Sister Halim. Two True Believers.

"Is that why you're here?" I asked him. "As a committee?"

"Ezra, are you all right?"

"I'm fine."

Yael smiled brilliantly. "And how is Maryam?"

"She's fine too."

"Talk to us, Ezra," Deddy said.

"And you'll make everything all right?"

"Sure. I have a plan. Haven't you heard?"

"When did you start having plans, Deddy? When did you get to be a rabbi?"

"Suppose we just get a drink?"

"Do rabbis drink? Or do you just get drunk by rubbing yourself against the flesh of the unwounded?"

Deddy's smile stayed fixed on his face. "So who's un-wounded?"

"I was up on the Golan again, yesterday. We're still there, Deddy. I could step back into the place we were as easily as going through a door."

A film of perspiration broke out on Deddy's face. He wiped it away and massaged his stump, like a consoling ges-ture to his body.

"In that trench, Ezra, in the hospital afterward, you pulled me back into life. But I feel helpless to do the same for you, to pull you out of whatever trench you're sinking into."

I raised the bottle. "Captain rabbi."

He got up. "I'll tell you what—if you like, call me to-morrow. I'll make everything better. I'll be a rabbi or a scapegoat, whatever you're looking for. Meanwhile, take it easy." He looked at Yael.

"I'm going to stay for a while," she said.

Deddy nodded. "Of course," he said, as if it were what he expected of the evening.

"You shouldn't do that," Yael said, when he'd left. "He's been worried about you. He's your friend."

"We're both such good friends of his, aren't we?"

She picked up the bottle and drank the last drop of co-gnac. "What are you taking out on him? Didn't you get to fuck that Arab?"

"You have a filthy mouth."

"Do I? I'm sorry. Sometimes I'm a rotten bitch. But I try not to be." She put her hand on mine, as if seeking my help in it.

We walked to Agrippas Street, through the crowds. The ac-tivity on the street was still strange to me, after the kibbutz.

Everyone seemed engaged in a frantic parody of a city. Eddies and currents of people swirled around us, groups bunching and unbunching to a rhythm I no longer felt. The mob was thickest in front of the Eden Cinema. When we passed it, the street became less crowded, less noisy. I began to feel bad about Deddy. I was just striking out at him, the way people threw bricks at him when he spoke at rallies, nagging them toward peace when what they really wanted was the hate they'd built their lives around.

Two boys, each wearing tight black pants and shiny purple shirts, appeared in front of us. The boys hugged each other in greeting, then backed off, spinning key chains in faster and faster circles, as if gauging the excitement of meeting each other. *"Ahalahn,"* one exclaimed with great satisfaction. "Good evening, Doctor Kissinger," the other smirked.

Yael put her arm around my waist. I draped my arm around her shoulders.

"Better," she said.

We passed the stalls selling *schwarma* and grilled hearts. The waves of heated air from the grills wafted the smells of burning meat and peppers out to us. Yael turned left, leading me onto a narrow street. We stopped in front of a two-story building. She opened a latticed iron gate. There was a small courtyard inside, paved with uneven stones. The second story of the building had a flimsily railed catwalk around it on the inside; the inner walls of both stories were lined with wooden doors and narrow, barred windows.

I followed Yael upstairs to the catwalk. The flat consisted of a single large room and a small bathroom. A half refrigerator, sink, and two-ring gas burner sat in an alcove. There was a sense of shared references about the way the place was furnished that was comforting, that I hadn't had at Jebel

Halim. A student's flat, with a bookcase made of two-by-
fours resting on concrete blocks, a green-glass Hebron vase
with dried thistles in it sitting on the top shelf with a line of
dusty paperbacks leaning against it, Camus and Sartre and
Arendt and Buber; a van Gogh *Sunflowers* poster on the wall.
Yael came over to me. Her blond hair was done in braids.
She was wearing a half-buttoned khaki blouse, darkened
with sweat: young Israel gone dirty.

She switched off the light. Her face and body showed
in the barred light from the window. Then that light went
out too.

"Where are you?" she asked.

"I'm here."

Her skin was sudden and cool against mine. We touched
each other and moved together. She fit herself to me, her lips
against my chest, murmuring words I couldn't understand.
In the darkness I clung to her, embracing a need to betray
love.

A light from a passing car glowed through the slat blinds,
then was gone. He rose on one elbow, sank back down. A
gleam of white sheet, the smooth length of his skin, prismed
glitters of sweat. Momentary points of light and then the
dark again, its heaviness expressed in heat. Like living under
a blanket. The irritating heat collected in the folds, nested in
the hollows and bunchings between us as it was nested in
the hollows and valleys of the city outside. Darkness folded.

"It isn't," he said aloud, to a dream.

What does he know? Does he think because he's here,
stinking of her rotten cardamom and straw and curdled milk
and acrid sweat smell that they all have, does he think he's
brought me light? Like Deddy, my crippled little light to all
the world. But I met Ezra in the darkness of a blackout.

He stirred. Who does he think he is with this brooding
drunk act? And his friend, the bleeding saint. Still defending
Ezra as if in danger of losing his other arm. Or his testicles.
Last night at the Nahlaot house, all of us lying around on
the floor like an orgy of impotents, the Painful Subject of

Ezra was Brought Up. Yonatan spoke for the Disturbed Majority. Listen, if he's not in, he's out. Who can trust him, Deddy? He's erratic. And that Galahad act at the American school didn't help. And while we're at it, we need to be doing more on our side of the Green Line. Forget the territories for now. Forget contacts with the Arabs. You found one Arab to talk to and she disappears. We need rather to show the public where we stand. We need larger demonstrations, to show to the world that these Gush fanatics aren't the country. Let's parade our goodness because we can't do anything else, why not say it? Sure, forget the Arabs, *boychik,* Deddy said. We'll make peace with the Danes; they admire us, it will be easier.

None of this quietly, in normal tones of discourse. Screams and stridency. Yonatan shouting, his neck corded, his eyes bulging. Everyone talking at once. Justice against justice. The dispute isn't symmetrical. Their response to our national tragedy. Real concerns about security. Choice between repression and compromise. The words and phrases all billowing with the clouds of smoke in the room, petrifying in front of my eyes into the fossil dust of chalk, like the sayings of the wise, the chachamim written carefully on school blackboards that David would laugh at while I memorized them solemnly, as if they were truly lessons I'd apply to my life. Remembering that the Existence of the Nation is in the Hands of the Youth on my way to the greengrocer. I trust in the future because I have kept before me the image of the past. Warriors are we, last in the era of bondage first to be free. And a pound of onions.

All of them talking at once, these chachamim, and thinking about what clever chalk-dust phrase to blow out next as if their purpose in life was to end up on blackboards, all of it to me becoming an incomprehensible noise, a part of the din of the streets and the market and the buses: an impossible level of noise and passion to live within. So I retreated from it. I let the thick smoke in the room turn into a veil and then into a wall that filtered the roar of noise to a whisper, to the muffled sound of a bloodthirsty crowd as heard through the thick walls of an arena by the victim waiting her turn to walk out onto the sand.

Later, they'd fallen asleep on the floor, spent from all the words and phrases they'd ejaculated, all of them circled around Deddy like spokes. But I sat awake. In the morning, the light started to come in through the slits in the metal shutters, first outlining, then filling in the shapes on the floors, the light spreading from the hub of Deddy giving substance to all those empty husks. And I knew that why I was there, part of the closing of that circle, was not because of any chalk-dust phrases (for now David sits in my womb, an unborn fetus in a half-empty sack, his bitterness flooding my veins) but because I needed to be a part of this community of husks, of the wounded. The light strengthened, a strange, bleeding light, Deddy's light: it made the house seem the last place at the end of the world.

But I met Ezra in the darkness of a blackout.

All day, through the hours of light, I'd sat next to David's bed in the hospital, reading a newspaper. The plasma jars above his bed clinking ceaselessly, like manic toastmasters. My eyes fastened to a boxed advertisement at the bottom of the front page. A beautiful woman, her eyes thoughtful under a wing of black hair, staring at me accusingly. I read the words under her over and over, like a prayer. Boost Their Morale. You are obliged to look beautiful, well-groomed, and pleasant. For you are the source of courage to our menfolk. For you are responsible, now more than ever, for a cheerful atmosphere at home. It may require an extra effort but keep smiling and try to look extra lovely. It will work; it will raise their morale. Helena Rubinstein. Beauty That Works.

The words of the chachamim. I read them over and over, clinging to the advertisement's firmness of tone, its strident promises in the face of David's continued silence. Its instructions. Finally the nurse took the paper from my hands and I understood that words had no power.

"You have to go," she said. "I'm sorry. We need the bed." Her mouth a black hole, dark with the darkness she'd sucked, flitting bed to bed. An Arab face. The face of my enemy.

"Try to look extra lovely," I told her. "It works."

"Would you like someone to take you home?"

In the darkness of the blackout, the long building of the hospital was a person sleeping uneasily: a thick shape that gave out groans, mutters, and gleams of light, as from half-opened eyes. I stepped into the blackout, into the folds of a blanket. On the street in front of me I saw three men in uniform. I knew immediately who they were. In the dark they couldn't see me. They stayed close to the sides of the building and didn't speak. I walked behind them like a ghost trailing the news of her own death. For that's who they were. The army sent an officer, a doctor, and a rabbi. One for each need. Patriotic, physical, spiritual. When people saw them coming they'd shut doors in their faces. As if they were three angels of death. As if their news could be stopped. But the army was merely being compassionate. Compassionate and efficient. I looked after the three, my hatred for them burning like a light strong enough to break the blackout. As if I'd set it off, the automatic hallway light behind a building door clicked on. A woman came out. She dropped her keys into her handbag and looked up at the three passing angels.

The skin on her face drew and tightened until she was standing in the doorway with her own death. Try to look extra lovely too, sweetie. It will work. She gasped and ducked back inside. The light in the hall clicked out.

We continued down the street, the three of them and me, their invisible ghost, representative of all the ghosts their words had brought. The other people on the street moved by us silently, lowering their eyes. They formed gliding, monkish processions. The city without light. The blackout covering everything like a thick blanket that held time in its folds. The darkened display cases in the Chen Cinema still advertising films that had been showing before the war. Like watches that had stopped the moment their owners died. A car gliding by with a subdued hiss, its painted blackout headlights splashing the street with an aqueous blue, drowning it, creating the balconies and facades of a sunken city. The light washing up the side of a building, carrying my eyes. On the second floor was a balcony. Two long glass cages were fixed on each side of it, fastened to the wall of the building. In one cage was a mannequin dressed in a bridal gown. Her hands reached out, groping blindly against the glass. The other cage was empty. The caged bride looked substanceless, an echo, beauty that didn't work. She cried out, an echo. My own, stupidly gaped mouth, caught her cry.

The three men turned around and looked at me, as if my cry had breached some etiquette. They stared in silence. Three soldiers staring at a girl. Three who now more than ever were responsible for the atmosphere at home. Could I boost their morale? I clutched my breasts and pointed them like guns, squeezing. They frowned and started toward me, their mouths dripping with words. A hand touched my shoulder. It was Ezra's.

And so we met.

"It's all right," he said.

"Listen," one of the men, Patriotism or Physicality or Spirituality, said. "We talked to her at Shaare Zedek. She needs to go home."

"It's all right. She's with me."

Pressing my shoulder. Leading me away. In his filthy fatigues. His face a blur in the darkness, an echo of darkness.

"Who are you?"

"I was in the hospital visiting a friend. I saw you there."

Did he follow me? A ghost following a ghost.

"I was walking this way. Listen, I'm sorry."

"About what?"

He looked at me helplessly. Wondering what he'd gotten himself into.

"About my brother?"

"Yes. About your brother."

"His name was David. Saying his name won't curse you."

He said nothing.

"Let me tell you something. When we were children, my brother and I, we were raised on partisan stories. We'd play at being partisans. It was what my parents were. Today they're back in their forest so they couldn't come to the hospital. My brother and I would slip through the forests and fight the fascists, moving like fish through the water of the people. I was always much better at it than him. Yet I'm a clerk, at Schneller. Does that make sense?"

"Let's get a drink," he said.

"I know a place," I said.

We walked through the blackout, the darkness nested in the folds of the city.

At the Gallery, women and a few men in filthy fatigues, like his, their weapons leaned against the tables, huddled like conspirators around flickering candles. The low hum of conversation stopped when they saw me.

"And isn't it terrible," I said to them, "that she came out tonight?"

"Come sit," he said, and guided me to a table.

"Have you been here before?" I asked. "No? You're not the café type, are you? You're not full of words."

"Let's have a drink."

I leaned on his arm. "Who are you, anyway? Part of the plan? Did they send you to me? Are you a fourth angel of death?"

I could hear him breathing heavily, as if I'd named him, and then a catch in it that caught in my chest and continued until I felt the whole blacked-out city, the silent, blue-lit, drowned processions shuffling along its street, freeze, all frozen forever in its folds of darkness.

A popular song about Jerusalem came on the radio. Full of words, like the sayings of the wise.

"Jerusalem of shit," I said.

I opened my eyes again. My bunched up sleeping bag lay
next to the sofa like the husk of a decaying insect, underwear
and socks scattered around it: its droppings. Bottles and
brimmed ashtrays everywhere, a fetid odor of mildew hanging in the air. This was no dream.

I went into the bathroom and used the commode. My
head felt crusted and gummy inside, full of poison. I let the
cold water run in the sink until it was icy, then drank deeply
and slapped my face with it. My skin felt numb, calloused
between myself and the sensation of the water. I looked into
the mirror, then looked away.

The turd-shaped piece of hashish Bashir had given me
was lying on the table. It was a compensatory gift: I'd started
working for him again, but the filming had been suspended
because of labor troubles. The Bedouin wanted more money,
and they and the Jericho Arabs were at each other's throats.
The film crew were impressed by the Bedouins' dress and
authentic customs and their desert skills—their ease and grace
of movement in the terrain, their handling of animals and

weapons—and the Jericho Arabs were resentful. In front of foreigners and cameras, the Bedouin were usurping some ideal image of themselves they could no longer claim.

I extracted a cigarette from the small olive wood box next to the hash, and rolled the tube between my thumb and forefinger, letting the tobacco spill into my palm. I lit a match, ran it over the bottom of the hash, kneaded chips of softened material into the tobacco in my hand, placed the empty tube of the cigarette into the mixture like a proboscis, and sucked in, concentrating on the details of the task. I twisted the end of the paper and regarded my work. I'd done it as well as any Bedouin could.

I lit the cigarette, inhaled deeply, and held the smoke in my lungs. The bookshelves in the room pushed in on me. Since I'd been back, I'd let my studies go to hell; I hadn't even checked back in at the Technion. The last two weeks had been drinking at the café until it closed at two in the morning and moving out into the street in a crowd, our shadows dancing crazily on the buildings. It had been Deddy and Yael standing in front of me, still a committee, telling me I was giving Breira a bad name and what was wrong? It had been waking up with strangers and parties in Musrara and Baka—smoking from broken bottles, the hash and tobacco stuffed into the jagged end and the neck thrust into a glass of wine and sucking the smoke from between the stained thumb and forefinger of the walleyed Moroccan dealer holding the glass for me as a sign of brotherhood. It had been with Bashir to the smoke shops of the Old City, where the ancient Bedouin next to me, planted on his stool, his nose a ruin of burst veins, wiped the mouthpiece of the pipe back and forth on his stubbled cheek to clean it before passing it to me and grinning terribly when I took it, the smoke raising me on a wave out of time and the circle grinning at me and my lungs raw. It had been the low, pressing roofs of the smoke houses and the security so good and my uncle's police so paid off that we'd be warned and know exactly how many times we could pass the pipe before we'd exit down the narrow stone steps and watch the police go up and we laughed at the game of it, at their stiff-shouldered posture and intent seriousness suddenly ridiculous so I understood that yes, the drug was a danger to the nation, and laughing, laughing and knowing suddenly how easy it would be simply to continue like this, lighter than air, a floating spectator, the opposite of some ideal image of myself.

Jerusalem of hashish and of dust. In my dreams it spun on its hills in malicious delight, pulverizing examples of Jebusite, Hebraic, Seleucidic, Hasmonaean, Roman, Herodian, Byzantinean, Caliphatic, Crusader, Mamlukean, Ottoman, British, and noveau Miami architecture, creating a strange pink light. In my dreams, it dreamed of herdsmen at dawn, like an image of itself it could no longer claim. It dreamed of its sediments of dead, shifting uneasily.

In my dreams, Walid Halim, poet, nationalist, head clerk of the Jerusalem YMCA, came to me.

Listen, I said to him. The city dreams of itself as but the earthly reflection of a heavenly city, its temporal battles as mere metaphors, parables, fables.

Walid Halim nodded wisely.

Thus it gets away with murder, he said.

Shit, sergeant architect, Deddy said.

Absolutely, captain policeman.

In all my imaginings I hadn't expected this: a short man in a green leisure suit, pock skinned and bald, his neck thicker than the top of his head, and the most intelligent, compassionate eyes I'd ever seen.

"Hello," he said. "At last, welcome."

I tightened inside myself, not allowing myself to forget (not allowing myself to sink into and drown in those eyes) the way I'd been kept isolated.

"To whom am I speaking?" I asked.

He sat down. "A correct response would be 'Welcome.' An Arab response." His voice was as gentle as his eyes, but edged. He relented with a smile that was like a shared secret between us—it isn't me who insists upon correct responses, the smile said.

"Why have you kept me prisoner like this—is this Arab hospitality?"

The smile remained fixed and reasonable on his face.

"Tell me, Maryam," he said. "Are you familiar with the Jewish Passover service?"

I shivered inside myself; it was as if there were two spectators watching me: Ezra, lean and sardonic and grinning at all these Levantine goings-on, and this man, who shared my secrets as if he'd been with me all my life, an eavesdropper listening to me, watching me, waiting for me to come to him.

"Yes," I said.

"Do you recall the portion in which the four sons ask questions and the wicked son asks, 'What do you mean by this service?' and is admonished for not including himself among the people who were liberated?"

"I do include myself."

"Are you sure?"

"Yes."

"Are you ready to follow orders, without hesitation, without reservation, without"—he rolled his eyes comically—"without *questions?*"

I was silent.

"I asked you a question."

"I have no stomach for killing."

He waved away my answer casually. "I didn't ask you to kill anyone. I want to know if you're ready to serve your people, to make sacrifices for your beliefs."

"Yes."

"Good. Then what I'd like you to do is rent a car."

He looked surprised at my surprise.

"It should be easy for you—you're a citizen of the enemy state, you speak the language, you have valid identification papers. What I want you to do is return, rent a car, and drive it to a certain place." He held up his hands. "Rest your conscience, I don't want you to leave anything in the car. No surprises. Simply bring it where you're told to bring it. Afterward, we'll get you back here to us." He crossed his hands on his chest, gathering me to his bosom.

"And you brought me out of the country, brought me here, just to tell me this? Why? If that's all you wanted you could have given instructions to me there."

He shook his head in exasperation at my questions. "I will tell you only that the car is important for a major operation. That's all you need to know. We have reasons for all our orders; you need simply to relax and accept that fact."

I needed to simply step into a shaft and let myself fall. "You mentioned that I have valid papers," I said slowly. "Why should that matter—won't I be given false identification?"

He raised his eyebrows. "Why? You have perfectly good documents."

"And if I use them they'll know who rented this car that's important for your major operation," I explained, as if I still believed it was a point he'd overlooked. His eyes widened slightly, registering his appreciation that I understood he wanted the car tied to me.

"A minute ago you said you'd make any sacrifice," he reminded me.

"I'm willing to sacrifice myself."

"But not others? Not which others, daughter? Your mother? She may be questioned, but that's all that would happen to her. What other sacrifices aren't you prepared to make? Your house? But that's simply stone, Maryam. And most of your people have no houses."

I didn't speak.

"Or do you mean Ezra Brenner?"

"Why do you bring him up?"

"Our man tells us you were with him at the pickup point," he said gently.

"He only gave me a ride—he wasn't there when I was picked up, and he didn't know why I was going there." I thought of Riad's warning to me, after he'd seen me running with Ezra. "No one in the village knows I left with him—Aida wouldn't say anything. Anyway, I don't see what this has to do with anything."

He looked at me blandly. "Oh, I think you do. You insist on continuing to ask questions. But you're afraid to hear the answers."

"I was instructed to form ties with Breira, with the group Ezra's a part of."

"Yes, and you succeeded admirably, even more than we dared hope."

I've read, my darling, of a form of execution in which heavier and heavier stones were pressed on the chest of the condemned until she was pressed to death.

"It's Breira, isn't it?" I said, putting the weight into words. "That's why you brought me here, brought me out under my own passport—so I'd leave a trail. That's why you want me to rent the car. You want my name connected to a terrorist act because my name's connected to Breira." I laughed shrilly. "You've been my matchmaker. But why? Who cares about Breira?"

"It's a pleasant mask over the face of a monster."

"It's simply a group that wants change."

"Better such groups don't exist. They only create confusion, obscure the intentions of the enemy—sometimes even in the eyes of our own people."

"It's not that influential."

"Its influence is growing. Last week, in Tel Aviv, thousands of people participated in a demonstration held by Breira—and some of those people were Arabs. Each time, Breira attracts more people. Each time, it confuses the issue more. Breira—alternative. But alternatives can paralyze us."

"Tying me to Ezra, to Breira, isn't going to destroy it."

"It may help. But you miss my point." He stared at me. "Israeli-Arab," he said. "Have you considered the impossibility of that term?"

"All my life."

He nodded. "It's not a description. It's a choice. And I want our people in Palestine to know the choice that the daughter of Walid Halim has made. I want them to know it clearly. The daughter of Walid Halim owes us that. Listen to me, Maryam. When you finally come to us, you're filled with qualifications and reservations. Use me, you say, but not too much, not so it hurts. But you can't come here without pain. You can't come here without paying your way with everything you have. Do you understand that?"

His eyes left me no place to go.

. . . . Ezra

There was always the Gallery. Its patrons tend to be what my uncle likes to call marginal people: a few underworld characters for color, but mostly writers and artists and dissident political types, all huddling together, breathing in one another's breaths and exhaling their own atmosphere, escaping the narrow ghetto of the country into the narrow space between the walls of the café. I needed the pressing reassurance of those high, yellow walls as much as any of them, the comfort of the margin, of being neither here nor there.

The fourth table on the right from the front door was mine. I had a place of honor across from Naftali, a burned-out ex–armed robber who sat slack jawed and dull eyed behind a wall of uncomprehending silence, like an illustration of the next stage in my drunk.

I drank far into a fine afternoon, working at blunting the jagged shards that seemed to tear around inside me whenever there was too much clarity. The shapes around me hazed, thickened, emerged finally as Bashir's grinning predator bird's face.

"You look terrible," he said.

"You look like a grinning predator bird."

Bashir sat down.

"Have a drink," I said.

"A Goldstar," he said to Nissim.

Bashir sat and waited for the beer. When it came, he sipped it and made a face.

"Do you have anything for me?" I asked.

Bashir put down his glass. "As in work?"

I pantomimed sucking in smoke from a cigarette. Bashir looked at me reproachfully.

"Ezra, you worry me."

"Are you part of the committee?"

"A committee won't help you, my friend."

"Are you another rabbi? Is that it? Rabbi Dealer." I squinted at him as if trying to make him out.

Bashir waved at the room. "And what picture are you, Ezra—in this Gallery? Love's dying fool? The maladjusted drifter? There are people around with worse problems. But they can't afford to be drunks and addicts."

"Neither can I. Buy me another drink."

Bashir looked away, a sickly grin twisting his lips. He couldn't help it; I was funny, a drunk is always funny. I felt sick also, a twisting, helpless sickness. He was right about me, and I was more than a little tired of my act also. But I didn't for the life of me know how to stop. Bashir was looking at Naftali. I watched his grin hook into Naftali's fierce, flat Genghis Khan face, its features blunted and softened now, spittle wetting the corners of its mouth. Naftali stood up, as if pulled by Bashir's smile, his lips involuntarily re-

flecting it, his face straining to get the joke. He shuffled over
to us, pulled by his idiot's grin. Bashir shook his head gently.
Naftali nodded, as if something immense had been commu-
nicated to him, and shuffled out.

"You're heading for that," Bashir said. "Naftali's your
Platonic ideal."

Naftali was one of the Oriental street toughs who'd
started the Black Panther party as a reaction against Ashkenazi discrimination; before that he'd been a successful armed
robber and extortionist specializing in the diamond trade.
Whenever there was a particularly spectacular robbery in Jerusalem or in the Tel Aviv diamond district, Naftali would
always be the first one picked up. He'd never try to get
away, but would simply let himself be taken to the Russian
Compound, where he'd be given all the usual "treatments,"
but never say a word. His silence, not to mention his body
and his head, was a rock, the training ground for a generation of police interrogators, the breaking point for their sticks
and boards. My uncle always spoke of him as a "tough Jew,"
the highest rank in Aharon's hierarchy of respect. When the
Black Panthers started, though, Naftali transferred all his or-
ganizational skills to the cause. Eventually, the Panthers were
bought off, by my uncle's informers, by their infatuation
with their own fame. They took to coming to the Gallery
far too often, basking in the praise of the café intellectuals,
who were thrilled to associate with real underworld *lumpen-
proletariat* become socially conscious. Naftali, who in his profession had had to develop a talent for seeing things as they
are, grew disgusted and left the movement, resigning one
day by clearing out the café with a chair brandished like a
club. The next week, a spate of robberies broke out in Jerusalem and Tel Aviv. The month after, once the interro-

gators were finished with him, Naftali left for America. A few months later he was back, somehow defeated, a husk who sat in a corner of the Gallery.

"Do you know what happened to him?" Bashir asked me. "No? Let me tell you about it. Naftali goes to New York, yes? He's overwhelmed—the buildings, the people. America. What's a poor Jerusalem Moroccan boy to do? Like any immigrant, he looks around for opportunities, and stumbles into the diamond district. Hasidim everywhere: black gabardines, earlocks, diamonds. He feels a glow—it's like coming home. So he checks out the situation—even though he's Moroccan, his Yiddish is fluent; he perfected it for his trade. It's a piece of cake, he decides: he knows the patterns and habits of his prey. During the next two months there's a series of daring robberies of Hasidic diamond merchants and couriers. Naftali does one hundred, two hundred thousand dollars' worth of business—stick 'em up, in Yiddish. The land of opportunity. Then a big score—over half a million in uncut gems. This is too much for some of the Israelis already operating in New York. Come in with us, Naftali, they say. I'm not an organization type, he replies. So one day they snatch him, tie him up, put him in a little room, and force-feed him hallucinogens. Mescaline, pure LSD, PCP, whatever. No beatings, no pain. No hose up his ass or clips on his dick or two-by-fours breaking his bones, like the police would do. Just drugs, until his fine criminal brain melted and dribbled out of his ears and he had no borders left. Then they let him go. And eventually he ended up back here, a piece of furniture that drools."

"What's the moral of this story?"

"There's no moral to the story, Ezra. It's a sad story for Naftali. His life didn't happen as an example for you. You have your own sad story." He drank his beer. "But we all have to do what we do best, Ezra."

"What's that mean?"

Bashir sighed. "It means that what you do best right now is live on your reputation. It's fast turning to shit, but not everyone knows that yet. It means I have something for you, Ezra—if you wish. I'd like you to bring your reputation and go someplace with me."

I nodded. "A small role in your gangster movie. I'm to fold my arms or flip a coin or pull out a very small knife and clean my fingernails, all the while projecting my war record like an evil aura."

"Do I amuse you, Ezra?"

"I'm all for the movies."

He sighed. "So is the commodity I'm buying. Fuel for art. For our never-ending saga, our Moses. Me and you, we'll do a movie out in the real world so we can keep the idiots who employ me going. Do you know what an Italian-American production is? Canned spaghetti. They're putting me under a lot of pressure, both the actors and the crew, for more and more commodity to help their flagging creativity. That's the way they talk. That's what I have to listen to."

"I hear you bring it over the border."

"Late-night raft trips, secret signals, hands across the border—I'm the hippie peace plan, right?"

"What's happening with your extras?"

"My extras are a large part of my headache—they all think they're in a movie too. Do you remember that fool Barzini?"

"The big Italian?"

"A few days ago, he took to strutting around the set in a pair of red bikini briefs. My Bedouin sheikh, Abu Jabar, claimed Barzini was offending his women and threatened to surgically remove the great lump these briefs barely covered. What he wanted, in the real world, was to have another *sulha,* another feast of reconciliation. He's even learned to say it in English: 'a fist, a fist.' It was my fourth one for him. He's made the great discovery that the foreigners like doing *sulhas,* it makes them feel they're in the Middle East. It makes my ass cold, all that sitting on the ground. I arranged the first one after the riot—Abu Jabar asked for the life of the boy who started it by coming between a Bedu and his lover—his camel. He settled for money. Now he creates incidents whenever he can in order to do it again. He'll ask for Barzini's balls; he'll settle for money, everyone will be happy. The black tent, the sheep on a spit, the sheikh on one side, the director on the other, with his solemn, understanding-the-Third-World face, me and my cold ass on the ground. It's a wonder I don't start smoking that shit myself. Listen, Ezra, to tell you the truth, I'm under a lot of pressure and I have a request to meet you, a fan."

"A sort of precondition, is that it?"

"If you don't want to come, I can manage without you. But it's not a place I like to go without someone to back me."

"I'll come. Why not?"

"Don't take it lightly—do you think Naftali found the bad guys to be funny Damon Runyon types? Take that as a moral, if you want one. Please. You know, you try my patience sometimes, but I love you as a brother."

"I know—and we can't choose our brothers." We both laughed, but the funny part was that Bashir meant it.

He had a jeep parked illegally at the door. We climbed in and drove to Baka. We parked in front of a tall stone house on a hill.

There were elaborate Levantine greetings at the door, *ahalahns* and kisses, as if everybody hadn't seen each other in years. I was greeted with great fanfare, then ignored.

The four men and one woman in the room disappeared and another man came inside. He was short and thick as a plug, with a great shock of black hair swept back from his forehead and large, upward-slanting eyes and nostrils: a werewolf in an open purple shirt with a gold Star of David glinting from the matted black hair of his chest.

"Ezra, Yoel," Bashir said.

We sat on wicker chairs on a balcony that was thick with potted plants, the air fetid and damp from them. Yoel did the trick with the broken bottle. He smiled at me, glancing at the mirror that had been fastened on the wall and patting his hair into place, watching himself talking to me, the whole framed scene.

"Here, hero," he said.

He extended the glass, his hand, with its black tufts of hair sprouting from its back and knuckles, covering most of the rim. To smoke, I'd have to kiss his hand. That was the idea of it. I bent down to it and sucked in the smoke, the wine in the glass bubbling. He nodded, glancing at the mirror, enjoying the picture.

"Hero," he said.

The smoke boosted me up and out to an edge, somewhere above the scene. I wondered if this was something my uncle had set up: an elaborate attempt at discreditation. Bashir operated only at my uncle's whim—giving information was the price he paid to be left alone. Hash paranoia. An image of Naftali pursued by black-robed Hasidim came into my mind, and I shivered. Below the balcony, a fat woman with a colored handkerchief around her head waved up at us. The werewolf put the broken bottle and glass down.

A police car rolled past the house, the faces looking up at us. When it was out of sight, the woman grinned, gold flashing from her mouth.

"The people in this neighborhood love me," Yoel said. "We're family here, *hamollah*. Do Ashkenazim understand such things?"

I smiled at him. A werewolf smile. I saw myself as a stranger in the mirror. Yoel turned to Bashir. "What have you brought me, Bashir?"

"Ezra," Bashir said. "Please sit here, relax. Yoel and I will do a little business; I'll be right back."

Off the balcony and around the corner. The green door
creaked when I opened it and someone cursed at me. The
small box of a room was lit in dim silver through the mirror,
which framed the scene on the balcony. Ezra, sitting, tugging at the knees of his trousers. A projectionist's booth, so
that instead of being filmed by the camera next to Aharon,
the scene on the balcony seemed cast, as if onto a screen. In
all the times I'd seen this room used, I'd never seen him here
personally. Aharon the director become Aharon the projectionist. His face blank. Simply waiting for me to say something. The patience of a camera.

"What the fuck are you doing here?" Aharon's little
ferret whispered to me.

I didn't reply.

Aharon looked at me and nodded, silently directing me
to answer. I smiled at him. He raised his eyebrows and turned
away from me indifferently, peering back into the one-way
glass. I might as well have been on its other side.

A tall, thin old man came onto the balcony. He was

wearing striped, stained pajamas. His face was pale and liver spotted. He ran his fingers through thinning gray hair.

"Your friend Bashir is very wise," he said. His voice sounded hollow and metallic; the microphone it passed through had taken the human quality from it and replaced it with the flat tonality of a machine.

"Why is that?" Ezra asked.

"Who is he?" I asked Aharon.

"Mythology," Aharon muttered, his eyes on his nephew.

"Nathan," the old man said. "My name is Nathan. Do you mind if I sit?" He sat down next to Ezra and stretched his legs out, his heels on the balcony rail. Performing. Of course I knew who he was now. Until this moment he had always been a myth, an unseen figure spoken of in tones of awe by the underworld, manipulating his dealers and pimps and whores and extortionists from some invisible throne of power. The Old Man, Yoel called him, or more simply, God. I felt a fall of disappointment in my chest: God was on the screen, performing on Aharon's command just like all the rest of us. "Why do you think you're here?" he asked Ezra.

"Yoel knows I have an uncle on the police. Perhaps he feels protected."

"I know your uncle also, Ezra." I felt Aharon stiffen next to me. "Once we protected each other. But that's not what Yoel wants."

"What does he want?"

"Oh, Yoel enjoys demonstrating your corruption. A nice Ashkenazi boy. A hero." God flashed a quick death's-head grin at the mirror. Aharon's little pet cursed: "I told you—"

"Shut up," Aharon whispered.

"Bashir knows that," God said, my name sounding strange on his lips, turned into a stranger's name by his machine. "He and I are experts on what people enjoy—we have to be, don't we?"

"And what do you enjoy?" Ezra asked. "Being the philosophical thief?"

I felt a flush of pride for him, for my Jew. As if he were a brother I had chosen.

But it's out of my hands, Ezra, brother, brother stranger. You have to understand how I stay in business, what the rules are. Souk rules, a *sulha* in which everyone concerned knows the real price but has to go through the theater of feigned offense and cold asses and the dramatic walking away and the director calling them back and everyone happy. Why do you think I told you that story? Are you subtle enough, or has my commodity smoked away your brains? But we understand each other—you're my Israeli, but I'm your Jew. Your Druze. Don't you remember, when I first met you, when I was in that border police unit, how we Druze would be used to break up Jewish demonstrations, so Jewish policemen wouldn't have to do it? Don't you know that both sides use the Druze and the Bedouin, the grains of sand in between, for scouts, for their knowledge of the dead ground in between? That's what I own, Ezra, that's my true commodity. Abu Jabar the Bedu and Bashir the Druze both understand how to appease the forces they're caught between, how to erect fantastical tents in the dead ground before the camera and fill them with hashish and mirrors and trinkets and dreams. And that's something I'd think you would know about, my Jew.

"It's something I can do." God shrugged, the gesture making him a caricature, a little, wizened Polish Jew in striped pajamas.

"I've heard about your talents," Ezra said. "If you're the same man. To me, you were a character in a fairy tale."

"And now here I am, in real life," God said.

"Are you why I'm here? Do you enjoy my corruption also? Are you here for my uncle?"

Next to me, the ferret gasped.

God laughed, a dry hacking sound, thick with phlegm. "Your uncle was always in love with the idea of having to kill his own compassion in order to function." He looked directly at the mirror and smiled his skull's grin again. "Are you like that also?"

I glanced at Aharon. I was enjoying this brief rebellion of his puppets, Ezra's reconfirmation of himself in my eyes. But Aharon's face remained expressionless.

"It allows a certain freedom," Ezra muttered.

"One takes what one can." God laughed again.

Aharon turned to me. "Go back in there now. Quickly."

Yoel was waiting for me at the door, cursing me under his breath. He had a briefcase. I handed him the payment. We walked out onto the balcony together.

"Here's what you take, for example," the Old Man said to Ezra, waving languidly at us. His voice, no longer filtered through equipment, sounded strangely loud, his Polish accent stronger; it was the direct experience of the Divinity. He nodded to Yoel. "Is everything satisfactory—all exchanges made?"

"Yes."

"Good. You see, we all have what we want, Ezra. As usual."

"The Lord giveth," I said, "and the Lord taketh away."

"Exactly," God said.

Yoel's brothers came back onto the balcony. One was very large and the other small and slight, but both had the same coarse dog's hair and vicious cur's temperament of Yoel—his *hamollah,* his litter.

"We're under the hospitality of the house," I said to the Old Man.

"What a charming concept."

I looked at him. It hadn't been scripted this way. Aharon had promised I could keep the commodity, but apparently another brief rebellion of puppets was occurring—this Old Man planned to keep both my money and my dope. I felt a twinge of fellow feeling, even as I thought about cutting his skinny throat: God was dancing a little on his own while all Aharon could do was watch, trapped in his booth. A charming concept. But it was my dope.

Ezra stood up and moved behind the Old Man. The movement was a flicker, a sudden flame of a man flickering out of the drunk.

"It can happen very quickly," he said. He put his hands on the back of God's chair.

"Always." The Old Man smiled, but he didn't move his head, not even a little. His neck was thin and pale as milk. I moved in front of Yoel. He and his dog-brothers had the same fixed smile pasted on their faces as I had on mine. As if we could still turn it into an elaborate joke.

"It's a very quick movement," Ezra said. "Reach and snap. We used to practice it in the army." He winked at me. Enjoying himself, enjoying the gangster movie. "Do you exercise your neck very much? Is it as strong as your mouth?"

"But how will you leave?" the Old Man asked, with detached curiosity.

"You wouldn't need to worry about that."

God laughed, his dead-man's rattle, and waved at the mirror.

"It's out of my control," he said.

. . . . M ARYAM

In Athens, I took the airport bus to Syntagma Square, where I was met by a little man who wore a black turtleneck pullover in spite of the heat, just so he could look like everyone's idea of a terrorist.

"When the operation is over," he whispered conspiratorially to me, "you'll come back, you'll stay with the group here for a while." He slid his hand over my arm and stroked it. "You'll meet the cognoscenti." I wondered if this was how the rest of my life would be, among people who could use words like *cognoscenti* without feeling ridiculous, and suddenly I missed Ezra again, remembering the two of us with our laughter, like our house against the world, and I felt a scissoring of regret so sharp that it almost made me cry out.

A room had been arranged for me in a small pension near the Plaka; as soon as I entered it I closed the door in the face of the representative of the cognoscenti, and spent half the night vomiting. I spent the next day inside, staring through my window at the Acropolis, as if my confinement in Beirut had convinced me that this was the only way to see foreign cities.

The following morning, sitting in Syntagma—*show* yourself, Black Turtleneck had instructed—I bought a *Time* magazine from one of the kiosks selling foreign publications, then sat at a table, ordered coffee, and read. Buying the magazine was part of my instructions also, and I thumbed through the pages, looking for a message. In the international news section, a small article about Breira had been circled with magic marker: a large demonstration had been held in Jerusalem. Deddy's name was mentioned, his war-hero background, the combat he'd shared with Ezra Brenner, also in Breira, son of the well-known member of Parliament, the famous founding father, deceased. The article seemed written about people I didn't know, about a place I'd never been.

After a week I'd had enough of Athens. It was a Levantine city and had ruins, but these similarities only made me miss Jerusalem more. I wondered if this was how it felt to be in exile, this hollowness at the center. Under all the Zionist rhetoric was there simply this, a two-thousand-year-old void that had to be filled at my expense? Athens was the place to feel that void. Its ruins were set apart, isolated from the flow of life in the city, pristine on a hill: a museum piece eroding in the polluted air. In Jerusalem, ruins, even the new ruins that my lover had helped to create, were built upon, around, lived over, continued. The people swarming in the Plaka were lively, and they were familiar physical types, but they stayed closed to me, smiled falsely, and sized me up for a hustle. If I stayed here all my life, I'd remain an outsider. All my life in Jerusalem I'd been made to feel an outsider also, in the place where I'd been born. But in Jerusalem everyone was an exile of one sort or another; Jerusalem was a place where exiles felt at home.

I was booked on an El Al flight a few days later. How safe was the national airline now?

When the coastline came into view, the tourists on board broke into cheers and Hatikvah, and I joined them with enthusiasm.

"Do you have anything to declare?" the pretty, khaki-uniformed girl behind the customs counter asked.

Watch me.

I rented a Ford Pinto at the Avis counter. Once I was out of the airport it seemed impossible that I'd ever left, that anyplace else had ever really existed. The rooms in Beirut and Athens were the white rooms of a dream.

I drove south. *You'll get a full tank of gas at the airport so your first stop has to be far enough away to be logical.* The Sonol station was just where I'd been told it would be. I pulled in and gassed up, then parked next to a green Fiat outside the rest rooms and went into the women's toilet. The woman waiting in the stall was blond and heavy. We completed the metamorphosis within five minutes, just as I'd drilled in a narrow closet in Beirut; the woman, suddenly dark and slim, helping me with the padding. *Nudi, Nudi.* Today I was to be a star. When she left, it was as if she'd taken more than my appearance with her. I had a sense of myself disappearing through the door. A blond stranger with panicked eyes stared at me from the mirror. *What's the use of coming in on my own passport if I'm to be changed to someone else?* I'd asked. *It's important that you come in under your own name,* the man in the green leisure suit said. *But you will be watched, Maryam, and we need to shake them so you can move around freely.*

I waited inside for five more minutes. *No more, no less.* The idea was that anyone following me would think I was switching cars and follow the woman instead. *We set up a decoy for your watchers, then you take the decoy's place.* Coming out of the toilet in my wig and padding, I felt ridiculous, playing for a probably nonexistent audience. *A star.* It occurred to me that maybe the whole masquerade had been made up for my benefit, a test like the useless messages Riad would have me carry just to make me feel I was doing something useful. I suddenly hoped so, hoped I was still simply being tested, a small walk-on role with only a few lines to say. Being back made everything real again, and I didn't want to think where my actions were leading.

I drove to the Galilee, then followed the border east. It took me until early evening to get to the village where I'd been told to leave the car. The huddled stone houses and narrow streets, the sweet-acrid smell of cooking lamb and open sewers took me in the same way the country had taken me, but even more intimately. This was mine. I followed the directions I'd memorized. Down the main street, then turn into the fourth street on my right. I passed the first, the second, the third. There was no fourth street. It had to be some trick of my memory or a misunderstanding. I saw an old man with a seamed, kindly face sitting outside the arched door of a teahouse. I rolled down the window and asked directions to the address I'd been given.

He walked over to the car, shaking his head.

"I'm sorry, daughter, there's no such place in this village." A look of real regret passed over his face, as if it were all his fault. He bent down close to me. "Park there," he muttered. "In the alley. Then come with me, Maryam."

I followed him around to the back of the teahouse. He took me through a blue painted door and up a flight of narrow steps to a small room with whitewashed walls. It had a cot with a blanket on it, a table, a washbowl, soap and a towel. On the floor near the cot was an empty copper vessel. A slightly hysterical giggle escaped me when I realized it was a chamber pot.

"You'll wait here," the old man said, weaving his hand around to create the last white room of my journey.

"And then what?"

"When we tell you, you'll drive the car you've brought someplace else."

"I was told only to come here."

"You'll go where we tell you. For now, you'll wait."

. . . . A H A R O N

Sitting alone in my office, I could hear murmurings from the
pipes in the walls, like the whispered secrets of the city. For
a few moments I allowed myself to drift with that line of
thought, a kind of reverie I hadn't engaged in since I was a
young man who imagined himself a poet. The poets of one
generation, my brother Amos once said to me, are the secret
policemen of the next, and he was right—my poetry had
become the daydreams of a secret policeman. He was right,
but he'd never understood how necessary secret policemen
are for poets.

I wrote the thought down on my desk blotter, then
looked at the words. They were too ambiguous. For the
protection of poets? For the protection of society from poets?
But it was only the ambiguity of the wording that kept the
sentence from triteness.

This uncontrolled nonsense running through my mind
was somehow relaxing, and I sat still, retreating into a sort
of blankness, a suspension of weight. A mood broken by the
noise of a door slamming and the words "subsistence pay-

ments" shouted out like a slogan of the bureaucracy. I sighed and turned out the light; turned on the projector. The film began at the place I'd stopped it. Ezra bending his face to Yoel's hand, a look of peace, the eager acceptance of punishment suffusing his features. I stopped the film, took it off the projector, and unwound it from the reel. I keep a large antimony ashtray, a deep bowl really, on my desk, its rim fashioned into the crenellations of the Old City wall—a gift from one of my informants, an Old City souvenir merchant. I touched a match to the film, holding it over the bowl, watching it curl and burn. An overdramatic, not to say poetic gesture.

There was a knock. I fanned the air with my hand, switched on the recording system in my desk, and called, "Come in." It was like Uri Navon to come early.

He's a tall, thin man who affects cardigans and the fussy, absentminded mannerisms of an English don; eccentricities, it is said, he copied from a sympathetic warden when he was a Haganah prisoner of the British. His affectations were like the signs or marks of a club I could never join—there'd been no gentlemen jailers when I'd been held in this prison, and members of my organization had been viewed by the British as cutthroats. Navon regarded my reverse snobbery, my resentment of my country's real ruling class, as my weakness; I regarded his tendency to pigeonhole me as his. He pulled a chair up to my desk.

"Would you like some tea?" I asked.

"Let's finish this unfortunate business, Aharon. I have to submit a report to the minister."

"What do you want to hear from me?"

Navon raised his eyebrows to register my choice of words.

"I want to know how you managed to lose Halim," he said. "You assured me if we let her leave the country, you'd be able to keep track of her when she returned."

"She came back under her own identity—there was no reason to risk spooking her by following her too closely. We assumed she'd simply be put back into place as a sleeper, activated only when she was needed. If not, then why establish the fiction of a tourist trip abroad, why let her come back openly, under her own name? Perhaps surveillance was too light. It wasn't my surveillance, it was Shin Bet's, but I would have done the same. And I do take overall responsibility."

"Yes, you damn well do." Navon nodded thoughtfully, as if we'd never before spoken of Halim's travels under her own passport and he was hearing all of this for the first time. I wondered if he were making his own recording.

"How did she manage to lose her watchers?" he asked.

"Watcher. Only one. It was simple, a clean switch. Halim goes into a toilet, another woman made up to look like her comes out. The watcher isn't close enough to tell the difference; the second woman drives off; he follows. When she got as far as Eilat, we decided to pick her up. We're trying to identify her now, without much luck."

"Suspects not living through their arrests seems to be becoming a hallmark of your department."

"She had a grenade."

He ignored me. "And now Halim is somewhere in the country, wandering free."

"We'll find her."

"After God knows what damage she commits. You had more than enough on her to make an arrest, Aharon."

I steepled my fingers and tapped their ends together slowly. "Is that the official line now—the line you're going to hang me out to twist on?"

Navon sat back in his chair and closed his eyes, as if he'd experienced a great wave of weariness. "You've insisted on waiting to pick her up from the beginning. You've had a case now for a long time, for weeks before you came to us."

"Elhannan?" I asked. "Is that where you got the information?"

He opened his eyes and blinked at me. "I dislike the man immensely; he's a viper, a sycophant. But you need to be able to cover yourself, Aharon. Why didn't you pick her up before?"

"We didn't have complicity in an act of terror."

"Did you want her to murder someone, so she could be hung?"

"We don't hang in this country."

"Don't be frivolous."

"Then don't play ignorant with me, Uri. You knew what I wanted from the beginning—and your minister agreed with my reasons. The Halim name means something. And the Halims are Israeli-Arabs. A very clear example must be made of them."

"I understand the rationales."

"You did more than understand, you and your minister—you agreed. Do you still? I need to know if I still have your support."

Navon waved it to me languidly. "As long as you find her again, and soon. I'm merely suggesting you have answers ready, Aharon. Because if she causes any damage before you get her, we'll certainly wash our hands of you. Is that plain enough?"

"She'll be found."

"Good." He added gently, "Of course we agree with you. An example must be set." He glanced down at his watch, then, as if it were an afterthought, asked, "Tell me, was your nephew ever warned about Halim's connections to the PLO?"

I reached over and flicked a nonexistent piece of lint from Navon's collar, a gesture I'd use on a suspect I was luring into complacency. Navon flinched at the sudden invasion of physical contact, just as a prisoner would.

"Warned by whom?" I asked quietly.

"I meant nothing by the question. Only after what happened with Halim, it's important to us that nothing go wrong—with that part of the operation."

"That part of the operation? Do you mean the discrediting of Breira?"

A warning flickered in his eyes. "For God's sake, Aharon, are you taping this? I thought we had an agreement?"

I spread my hands. "Would you care to search my office?"

"Don't be ridiculous." A fine line of sweat had formed on his forehead. The don was a prisoner of his own good manners.

"Tell me, Uri, does Breira ever remind you of your own shining youth? Of your dormant conscience?"

Navon looked at the ceiling.

"It doesn't remind me of mine either. But then you know all about my youth, don't you? I had to put aside my conscience so that people like you and your minister and Breira would have a place where they could exist and agonize about theirs."

"Are you running for Knesset, Aharon?"

"Neither of us is. So put it into words, Uri. Tell me what this is about."

"You know we've had concerns from the beginning about your involvement. To put it as bluntly as you seem to want me to, we're worried about your ability to handle your feelings towards your nephew."

"I don't have a nephew."

"How dramatic. Are you going to rend your clothing, sprinkle ashes on your head?"

I reached into the bowl, feeling the slick, faintly moist ashes between my fingers. I smeared my forehead with them. Navon reached over the desk and grabbed my arm. "Aharon." His voice cracked with panic. A place in time held securely in his mind—office, gray furniture, two men of easy power, their pasts comfortably buried under softened flesh and soft years—had suddenly disintegrated. A building, always there, a landmark, had been demolished in an instant. Terror. There was no permanence and therefore no trust in permanence: the dynamiter as the social and psychological equivalent of cancer. A balloon of pressure pumped up behind my eyes; it pushed Navon's concerned face away from me, behind an invisible wall of distance and silence, his eyes small staring dots, fastened to me. I saw myself through them; my action the unbalanced, impetuous gesture of a Stern Gang poet. Why not? Halim had finished me; I was liberated from the policeman, liberated from permanence: I had again the freedom of the terrorist.

"The crime of knowingly meeting with a member of a terrorist organization carries a twenty-year sentence," Navon said slowly, his eyes sliding away from my face and its mark of ashes, choosing not to see. "Are you prepared to do that to your nephew?"

I leaned in closer to him, bringing my face near his.

"I'm hairy Esau again, aren't I, Uri? You don't want anyone to know you have a killer in the family, but you want me to do my job, don't you? Don't worry—I won't connect you or your minister to it. But I'll give you Breira."

Navon looked at me with distaste. And said nothing.

. . . . MARYAM

The night would never end. A strong, cold wind was blowing down from Lebanon, pushing dark clouds in front of the moon in skittering eclipses, rattling the car. It was insane to wait like this. I could just leave the keys in the ignition and go. You won't do that, the old man who never gave me his name had said. You'll sit and wait. Sit in whatever shadows I could find, exactly a kilometer and a half from the turn-off sign. Sit and watch the moon pouring liquid silver over the mountains. It was too bright for a crossing. They'd have to wait for clouds, like the clouds scudding over now, to darken the moon.

I'm a watcher on a hill. I sit staring at the swelling gray waves of the sea, watching the moonlight lace and sparkle on them, straining to see the dark, solid bulk of the ship bobbing on the water. I sit patiently; it all depends on me. When I spot the ship I'll radio my comrades and we'll wade laughing into the surf, grab the arms of the refugees, help them ashore. They'll see us, strong and tan and young, laughing as if it's all a child's game, and they'll weep for joy and kiss the wet sand. We'll take them into the hills and dance in joyous circles. We'll light triumphant signal fires across the land, in bright defiance of the British.

What I needed, I thought, on my hill far from any sea, was a Haganah to belong to, but all I had to choose from were Sternists and Irgunists. I felt a sudden chill: the references of my life, the wishful analogy I'd been using them to construct, were like a crack in a door I refused to look behind. Behind the door were faces. Those who would come over tonight didn't know those faces as I did. They saw instead the faces of the people in the refugee camps, strangers to me; they saw their women and children dying under the bombs and napalm, and the features of their enemy were blurred propaganda poster caricatures: cowardly murderers, skulking thieves, grasping Jews. But I saw other faces, familiar as my own. I shouldn't, but I couldn't help it: I'd grown up with them, and the face of my lover was among them.

But it didn't matter. I was just a driver. I didn't even know what the men I was to pick up tonight would do. Maybe they were on a mere intelligence-gathering operation: they would take pictures and samples of soil and leave. Or perhaps this night was only more of the test: the man in the green leisure suit would appear suddenly, smiling: Congratulations, daughter, you've proven yourself, now no more cowboys and Indians—I'm here to take you back to your real work.

I was dying for a cigarette. But it was another thing I'd been warned against. The glow could be seen for a great distance at night. And what about a forty-five-hundred-kilo car—how far could that be seen? I reached up and unscrewed the interior light bulb, then opened the door and got out.

Cold. The wind knifed my bones. Trees moved on the crests of the mountains like fringes of dirty black hair. If I went over that rise, I'd be invisible and I could watch the car in relative safety. And revolutionary discipline? The hell with it. We of the Haganah aren't robots; we pride ourselves on our initiative, our intelligence, our ability to adapt.

I was on top of the rise now. In the darkness gathered near the border I could hear the sound of running water, like the tinkle of bells in the wind. Perhaps a stream went under the fence near here. If it did, that would probably be the place where they'd come over. I lay down on my stomach, listening, straining to see. A cold spot, cold as ice, as death, touched the back of my neck and spread through my veins like some metastasizing doom. I rolled over. The man behind me raised the gun he'd put on my neck. No face. A black-and-white checkered keffiyeh wrapped around his head. Khaki shirt. Straps and bandoliers. His clones, two of them, appeared behind him.

He whispered, "If we were an army patrol, you'd be dead or captured."

"The car is over there," I said.

"Lower your voice and show us."

They were silent behind me as we walked; the weapons and equipment they were carrying were strapped down efficiently and barely made any noise, save an occasional creak. There was something familiar about the man's voice, the way the three of them moved, like parts of the same body. I knew them. I'd been their companion; we'd had photographs taken together. Dear Ezra, Having a great time. Guess who I met?

"Faster," the man behind me whispered. The boy. I remembered how young their faces had looked.

At the car I hesitated, then tried to hand the boy the keys. "You drive," he said, and I almost giggled—I'd been chosen for the mission because I was the only one old enough to have a driver's license.

But once I was behind the wheel, I didn't move. The boy looked at me impatiently.

"I was told only to bring the car here. Why must I go with you?"

The boy unwrapped the lower part of the keffiyeh from his mouth and jaw. "Just drive. I'll tell you where." He finished taking the headdress off. In the mirror I saw the two in the back doing the same.

We skimmed along the border. A truck passed going the other way, its tires whining. Another. The next car that passed had only its fog lights on, and the next had no lights on at all. If I kept driving on this road, I'd meet a patrol or a roadblock and they were undoubtedly looking for this car. The old man had changed the plates and repainted it, but surely that wouldn't be enough. I realized I was holding on to this thought like a hope. The traitor inside me. Sunlight began to strike the flanks of the mountains. I wondered what the sight did to the boy next to me and those in the backseat: their first view of the homeland was of a country bathed in fire. But they said nothing, only looked annoyed at the strengthening light. Maybe I was only to deliver them to a point where they'd be picked up by another car, to be smuggled deeper into the country: I was just the first link in a chain. I drove around a curve, too fast, and a sign appeared on the shoulder of the road: Hebrew, English, and Arabic letters spelling out the name Kfar Maya'an.

"Turn here," the boy said. "And slow down."

I drove toward the town. The wind had swept the sky clear of clouds. It would be a spotless day. The town was on the side of a mountain, and the wind sharply defined the lines of its white buildings. I saw each one clearly, as if through a lens. Then I was in the picture. The streets were deserted. Maybe people had been warned of our coming and had gotten out and it was all a trap. Laundry flapped against the sides of the buildings: empty sleeves and head-less shirts danced like mocking ghosts. An entire family hung on one line, done in underwear: a girdle, floppy boxer shorts, a pair of red panties, a smaller, more modest pair, three progressively smaller pairs of Jockey shorts. I drove up a hill, passing a town center that consisted of a sparsely grassed square, three sides of it bordered by a cloistered sidewalk lined with shops. An appliance store with discounts for new immigrants. A sick fund clinic. A beauty shop, a greengrocer, a falafel stand. The familiarity of it squeezed my heart.

The street followed a ridge line. The reality of what was happening was growing on me with the morning light. I couldn't move my foot from the pedal or my hand from the wheel: the bumps on it were cutting into my palm. The boy next to me was wrapping the keffiyeh back around his head; I heard the snick of a bolt sliding home, the murmur of a prayer from the backseat. On the slope of the hill below I saw an old, brown-skinned man chopping wood, the sound of his ax ringing against the mountain. Look up, I begged him, see us. He didn't. I was close enough to him and was driving slowly enough to see the cords of muscle working on his thin, strong arms. The sense of the ordinary in the scene mocked me. The old man chopped faster and faster, as if performing a daily magic that would bring the silent town to life, people its streets. Stop, I pleaded.

I was coming up on a block of apartment buildings. Characterless and blocklike, with balconies pulled out from them like drawers. Something vulgar that didn't fit into the landscape. The wood-slat blinds on all the windows were closed, some of them rattling in the wind. The boy told me to stop.

I sat, turned into a stone, weighted with dread. The boy said, "Come with us, quickly."

I didn't move. "I was only to drive you," I whispered. "I was only to bring you a car."

"Come," the boy said.

Then he was gone. The seat next to me was empty; the nightmare was over. Someone yanked open my door, and an iron hand gripped my arm and pulled me out, a reluctant, unready fetus. I suddenly had to piss; my bladder was bursting. They were dragging me between them, running, their footsteps echoing the rattle of the slat blinds. Into the hall. It closed around me, squeezing out the light. The boys gathered at a door and one pounded on it with the butt of his weapon. "Open," he yelled in Hebrew, "we're the police." The words came out stiffly, the phrase memorized. I heard a flurry of movement behind the door, but it remained closed. I tried to force my will against the other side of it, to keep it that way. The boys began running down the hall, pounding on doors and screaming like schoolboys playing a prank. The doors were blank, mocking expanses.

"What is it?" a sleepy, annoyed voice asked. The boys spun at the sound and fired. The door they hit flung open wide. They were screaming when they fired, and they didn't stop. I screamed with them. I saw gouts of blood on the door, trailing to the body heaped at its base. A small boy appeared over it, his eyes wide. They shot him, swept him away. I could see the inside of the apartment, its details magnified: shabby furniture, threadbare rugs. An insanely clear part of my mind wondered if it looked as pedestrian to the three boys as it did to me, if it was worth the price they were paying to enter it, possess it. A nightgowned girl, black hair flying, ran across the room inside. Their bullets followed her and slammed her against a wall, then dropped her, broken. Something from her head bubbled onto the white wall. A woman out of a nightmare leapt at me, the O of her mouth burning into my forehead and possessing me forever. The woman burst past me. One of the boys knocked me aside. He stood, feet planted apart, and fired, bringing the barrel of his weapon up in a steady rise. The woman flew for a few meters in the same direction she'd been running, then dropped heavily to the floor, as if this defiance of gravity had taken everything she had. Hands were grabbing me again. I let them pull me over the body, onto the slippery steps, into the street. The three boys got into the car. I stood outside.

The boy behind the wheel leaned through the window and brought his face close to mine. His eyes were bright and insane.

"Serve your people," he said.

He drove away.

I stood by myself. I could see the woman's body in the doorway. I clutched my own breasts, stomach, legs. I was wet with blood. With urine too, I noticed dully; my bladder had emptied. I vomited, trying to void completely, empty myself of the pictures. People were running toward me, surrounding me, their familiar Jewish faces, my lover's face, transfixed with horror and rage. They put their hands on me. They would tear me to pieces. I welcomed it: an end to the broken film loop that was repeating over and over in my brain: the woman running, flying to pieces, coming back and running again. But they were stroking me, murmuring soothingly to me, bearing me off: they thought I was one of them.

I cleaned and scrubbed the apartment in a flurry of nervous energy. A bottle of Red Label stood on the dining-room table, mocking my efforts like a bad companion who knew my true ways. The sight of it made my throat constrict with need. But I was sick of myself, of the wise-guy drunk, the dummy I'd created. I put the bottle in my dresser and took a shower, letting the icy water fill my open mouth, soak into my skin. Then I dressed and went to look for Deddy.

He wasn't in the Nahlaot house or at the Gallery. The former was deserted, and in the café the few customers looked at me strangely, then turned away tight-lipped, as if my decision to extract myself from them were a betrayal written on my face. I decided to try Yael's apartment.

When she opened the door, her eyes widened with shock. She searched my face. "Are you all right?"

"Yes, why not?"

She stepped back and I came inside.

"Have you seen Deddy?" I asked.

"He's out doing damage control."

"For what?"

"You didn't hear?"

She was drawing it out deliberately. The craving for a drink began to gnaw at my throat.

"Hear what?"

She looked at her watch. "They've been giving it every fifteen minutes." She went over to the table and turned on the radio. The Voice of Israel broadcasting from Jerusalem. I listened to it, and then I reached over and turned the radio off. Yael's eyes were glistening with a malice that hung on me like weight.

"Say something," she demanded.

"What do you want me to say?"

"Anything," Yael said. "Say you hate her, say you can't stand what she's done."

I reached over and brushed her lips with my fingers, erasing her words the way I'd once seen Deddy erase them.

"Enough," I said. It was all I could come up with, the best I could do.

I wasn't sure why I got out of the *sherut* in Ramat Eshkol. The northern edge of Jerusalem, its boatlike jutting into the Judean hills. But walking into them would be like walking off the edge of the world. For an insane moment I thought about going to Ezra, as if he were rest, sanctuary, as if he wouldn't shoot me himself. I was walking by the apartment buildings he'd once described to me as embodiments of political architecture, built to put a Jewish crescent around the northern border of the city. Art reduced to the service of politics, he'd said, produced only grotesqueries. Stereo sets with huge speakers, kitsch blared against the horror vacui. But they simply looked new and clean and comfortable to me. I wanted to go into one of them and go to bed. Pound on a door. Let me in, I'm the police. I took the flesh inside my mouth between my teeth and bit until I tasted blood. What can I tell you about it? I still have the illusion I can let you share my journey, bring you with me. My journey was art reduced to the service of politics. It reduced the scenery to kitsch. How did I get here? I'd allowed myself to step into a shaft and I fell. What can I tell you? I'll send you a postcard. Wish you were here. Wish you'd been there. When I needed you. You or a strong woman to take me away to the country of the women's room because I was stained like that, stained and leaking with my flow and that of my victims. But this time they'd taken me to the emergency room. The emergency room at Afula Hospital. It was a room filled with confusion: shouting people, hovering nurses, doctors screaming orders, and no one noticed me when I walked out and into a hallway. There was a laundry cart against the wall; I delved into it and pulled out a nurse's smock and went to the sanctuary of the rest room, washed my hands and face, costumed myself again, covered my shirt with the smock. When I walked out of the hospital, a few people looked at me, curious about a nurse leaving during an emergency. But no one stopped me. I went to the hospital bus stop and took the first bus into town. That simple. A line of *sherut* taxis was waiting outside the terminal. "Jerusalem!" a driver yelled at me, like a command. I got into the front seat. A small plastic trophy on the front dash announced to me that the driver was the World's Greatest Lover. He stared at me, at my clothing, my face, then smiled, his smile full of a dirty, secret knowledge. He asked me if I had any money.

I reached into my breast pocket, under the smock. I had money, identification, everything I needed to pretend to be a human being.

The backseats of the *sherut* filled up quickly. The other passengers were all men, rough voiced, dressed in blue kibbutz work clothing, each of them carrying an Uzi. They talked in hushed, reverent terms about Kfar Maya'an. I began to tremble. The driver looked at me again, grunted, started the car. We swerved onto the road. I felt the weight of a hand on my shoulder and shuddered under it: I had the vision that the woman in the apartment had grabbed me. A taxi driver in Jerusalem had been grabbed from behind and strangled. These were blue-clad sayaret agents behind me, agents of vengeance; they knew who I was, they were my executioners. The hand remained on my shoulder; when I turned I saw a tough, open kibbutznik face, looking at me with concern.

"Are you well?"

The genuine worry and kindness in his voice tugged away the last brick. I turned back around quickly, my eyes filling.

"Thank you, I'm all right. Just very tired."

His hand patted me. "It was a terrible thing."

I leaned my head against the window. The driver had turned the radio on and I heard the beep-beep announcing the news. I closed my eyes. Tracers flew across the inside of their lids.

There'd been a roadblock set up at the Green Line. I started to take out my ID, feeling relaxed, grateful that it would be over as soon as they saw my name. A soldier peered in. I saw suddenly what he'd see: a car full of armed kibbutzniks and a pretty girl. He waved us through.

To Jerusalem. To its northern edge. To you.

I walked between the buildings, a chorus of dogs marking my progress, until the city ended in a sea of blackness, the dark waves of it edged and frozen by silver moonlight.

I walked down the hill, off the edge of the world.

I kept to the wadi bottoms, staying in the darkness they'd gathered. The country funneled me in the right direction. I remembered running in it with Ezra. Thinking of him was a kind of anchoring peace, like the peace of knowing that

Jerusalem, the city where I'd been a child, was behind me on its hills.

I felt fever bright; surely I could be seen for miles.

Someone swore. I heard the creak and clank of equipment. I stopped. There was a clatter as if someone had tripped, muted laughter, a sharp command that halted it. I'd simply stand here until they came. I pictured the shock and revulsion spreading over the faces of the kindly kibbutzniks in the *sherut,* over Ezra's face. I wasn't ready, not here, not yet. I wasn't ready to serve my people. To simply rent a car. To be a slogan and a rallying cry. To rip off the pleasant mask. To change costumes again. I felt a surge of rebellion. Today I won't be a star. I didn't want to surrender; not to either side. I was filled with qualifications and reservations. I'd paid with everything they had and it was too much. The man in the green leisure suit had paid with everything I had and it was too much. Off to my right was an irregular shadow, lying between two boulders, opposed to shadows the moon was making and a deeper black. Closer, I saw what I expected: the entrance to a small cave. I went into it, feet first, as if I were drawing on a garment.

Or into a cocoon. The cave cocooned me. Wombed me. Its air was hot and fetid, dampened by the moisture coming off my body. The noise that the soldiers were making grew louder. Then the sounds passed me and faded. I lay still for a long time. Insect chirps, whirs, and the howls of jackals drifted into the cave. A small scorpion appeared in front of my face, its tail raised in threat. It danced for me in the moonlight, then scurried off, rebuked by my indifference. I lay still, feeling safe as a child in this earth folded around me.

. . . . EZRA

As soon as I walked back into the Gallery and sat down,
Nissim brought me a bottle of cognac and a newspaper. I
didn't refuse either.

I hadn't touched the newspaper, but I was about halfway
through the bottle when Deddy walked in. He sat down at
my table with a sigh. Nissim brought him a glass. He rocked
the cognac I poured into it back and forth, then gulped it
down.

"Did Yael tell you I was here?" I asked.

Deddy looked down at the newspaper. He ran his fingers
tentatively over the photograph on the front page. Maryam
standing with three smiling young men in keffiyehs, their
arms draped around one another.

"We need an etiquette, Ezra. A new etiquette for a new
age. Do we talk about her, have a wake—pretend we're
Irish?"

The words in the article ran from my eyes, familiar as
the litany of a prayer. A mother, father, and two children
killed in their home. A school taken over. Children from

another town on a field trip, sleeping in the building. The building wired to explosives. Demands. Deadlines. The army had to attack. The terrorists killed. Guns turned on the children. At least twenty dead. The people of the town trying to tear the bodies to pieces, the immediate retaliation in Lebanon—a camp hit by planes with no report of the number or kind of casualties. Maryam Halim. The terrorists' car traced to her. Disappeared. Her association with the Breira peace group. Her father's books.

"Swiss," I said.

"No," he said, looking at the headline. "We're Irish."

I tapped the paper. "They'll take it out on Breira."

"We'll survive. How about you?"

"I'm fine."

He grinned fiercely at me, a smile in a face lined with the pain of wounds, the face of a compassionate clown. He raised his glass. "To etiquette," he said.

I raised my glass. It left a wet circle on the photo of Maryam. Disappeared, the article had said. She was no longer on the surface of the planet, no longer held by the weight of the atmosphere. I knew suddenly where she would go.

"I'm all right," I said. "I'm just thinking of leaving the planet for a while."

He looked up at me quickly. "What?"

"I'm thinking of going out of the country."

He flicked his finger against the side of the glass and said nothing.

"Aren't you going to lecture me?"

"I wish you would stay," Deddy said, and we both laughed.

. . . . MARYAM

I woke up to a sharp pain in my side. When I rolled over it pressed into me and I could feel its shape, an edged shard between my ribs. I touched myself and my hand came away wet and there was wetness on the floor of the cave where I'd bled onto the rock. I crawled outside, blinking. There was a tiny hollow in the rock near the opening filled with rainwater. I cupped my hands into it and drank deeply, gulping down the stony-tasting water, then slapping it on my face. I pressed my shirt into my side, but I didn't want to look under it for the source of the pain. There wasn't much blood, but the pain moved sharply under my skin, the numbness leaving my flesh somehow connected to the changes in the rocks around me, their cool grayness drawing amber from the light, a color that I knew would strengthen and nimbus out of the stone to stain the air. I knew it because these were my rocks around me; I was close to home, too close. A peal of bells broke from the city, wild laughter. A goat brayed obscenely, like someone who knew a dirty secret about me. I cleaned myself the best I could, and walked back into town. That simple. No one stopped me, Riad, do you see?

At a kiosk on Herzl I saw my face in all the newspapers, surrounded by three heads in keffiyehs. In Kfar Maya'an they'd worn the cloth wrapped around their faces with only a slit opening to see through, the point of view of a weapon that sees only a target, that doesn't see the details of textures and colors or underwear on a clothesline or the shabby furniture of a life. And their faces, in turn, unseen also, only black eyes gleaming through the slits, the faces of weapons and not the cluster of pimples constantly worried and squeezed on a forehead, the film of perspiration, the soft tissue of lips kissed by other lips, the graceful curve of a cheek caressed by a hand, none of it, nothing of what they were. No one noticed me. Do you see, Riad, how easy it is to move among them?

I walked to his apartment building. The slat blinds on the windows rattled faintly, a shiver of warning at my approach. The front door was a blackness I couldn't bring myself to go into. I went around to the back, into the garden. No one stopped me. I looked through the glass of the patio door. There was no one in the living room. The door was unlocked.

I went inside. Emptiness and silence. Dust glittering in the air. I sat down in a padded chair, its softness cradling me. There were no changes in the room to register the changes in me since the last time I'd been here. Bookcases. Trotsky and the Jews. Medieval art and the Jews. Maryam and the Jews. Soccer trophies. Awards. Medals from his wars, for serving his people. A red-and-white keffiyeh draped over a lamp. Another trophy? Of his wars? Of my blood, the blood of my loins, that he refused to see? A silver samovar. His mother on the wall. Shostakovich and tea. A fragile vulnerability. An image of myself pounding on the door with the butt of a weapon, spraying Ezra with bullets, breaking him against the wall of books. The smell and warmth of his body clung to the chair. Waves of fatigue swept through me. Through a mist, I saw Hannah Brenner looking down at me, disapproving but determined to be tolerant. I wondered what she saw.

I got up and went to the bathroom. In the mirror my face was pale, and there were dark-veined translucent pouches under my eyes. I looked into my eyes, then turned quickly away. They stared back at me without mercy. I forced myself to look again. What if the reflection were an independent, malevolent entity? I distorted my face, and the reflection moved its lips back and bared its teeth. The eyes narrowed and mocked. I opened my mouth. The reflection rewarded me with an idiot's gape. What I was doing was of course feeding on itself. Are you sure? the eyes asked me. I turned away from them. When I looked back they were staring at me with hatred.

There was a roadblock on the way to Jebel Halim. A tall, blond *samal* came over to my window, smacking a clipboard against his leg, and asked for my ID.

"The area is closed," he said.

I nodded, then did a U-turn under his stare. Over a rise, I turned off the road and bumped down into a wadi. I followed it around a hill topped by an olive grove, then onto the path where I'd run. I stopped and got out. The village was on the other side of the next hill. I walked around its flanks, staying in the shade of the overhanging rocks, then up the slope to Jebel Halim.

In the main street, small prayer groups were gathered around transistor radios, listening to the news about Kfar Maya'an. I heard the name of the town and Maryam's name joined triumphantly in the midst of a stream of Arabic that went too fast for me to follow. The people listening to the radios turned away when they saw me, their faces closing, but no one came near me. PLO flags had been painted on some of the walls as well as slogans in Arabic and, as a goad,

I suppose, in Hebrew. Each phrase had Maryam's name in it. She'd finally found a way to bury herself in the heart of the village.

I went into the grove. It was empty. I walked to the oak. No one waited there. The thought that she'd be here had been crazy, a delusion. What would I do if I found her? I could see the house through the trees.

A cloud of dust rose from the hills, and I heard the sound of motors. A convoy of jeeps, six-by trucks, and half-tracks was winding down the road toward the village. If I'd arrived a few minutes later, I wouldn't have been able to come here through the hills. I stood rooted, watching, understanding suddenly why I had come, what I'd needed to see. I could anticipate their movements, the movements of a drill that over time had entered my body and become a tremolo in my bones and blood, a part of the pulse I could feel beating behind my ear. A pincher movement flanking to the left and another to the right, closing off. The troops rushing out of the trucks and half-tracks. The barricades up. The crowd hovering like a silent cloud behind them, quickly assuming its position, everyone on their marks, ready to be called back to do it again.

"Don't move."

They pointed their weapons at me; the sunlight sheening off the lowered plastic visors of their helmets, their heads faceless, insectoid. I raised my hands.

"Take your ID out and throw it over here. Slowly, you son of a whore."

I took out my wallet, showed it to them, and threw it over. A jeep pulled up, and two other soldiers jumped out. They began unloading equipment. The soldier who'd picked up my wallet raised his visor and looked at my card. He had a young, scared face.

"Ezra Brenner," he read out loud. "And what the fuck are you doing here, Mar Brenner?"

One of the soldiers who'd gotten out of the jeep walked over. He peered at me curiously, then grinned. "Are you joking?" he said to the boy with my wallet. "Ezra Brenner? Don't you remember—from the training films?" Smiling at me almost shyly, he held out his hand.

So I turned my back on him and on them and I walked into the grove, passing the piles of my possessions that they'd placed outside the barricade: the clothing and furniture and books and objects taken from the shelves—where was Aharon to tell me to leave my window open? I'd left only the photographs behind. The TV set was on a small table, its tubes and wires exposed like the insides of a person; the soldiers had taken it apart as if they expected to find my daughter inside. More piles of books, two beds, chairs and a sofa, pink as body organs. When my husband's cancer had spread, the doctors at Hadassah began scouring him out, part by part, leaving a husk, making a hollow that they could at last fill with themselves.

I walked to the edge of Jebel Halim, where I'd once stood unseen and watched the two of them running like children through the hills, just as I'd once stood unseen in a doorway and watched three children play on a roof, making a border their plaything. The air was still and hot, the sky so hard a blue it looked annealed to the horizon. On the slope below,

a wrecked car was rusting among the rocks and thistles. Its
metal looked brittle in the last strong light of day, as if what
was under the surface had fallen to dust, leaving only a light
shell to rest on the land.

I looked back, my eyes drawn unwillingly to the house.
The walls looked on fire in the last sun. But I felt nothing;
it was scoured and hollow, a husk they could fill with themselves; all my rage was dead, dulled under the soft weight of
children: three children who'd played on a white, dusty roof
and two children who'd run in these hills I turned my back
to now, and the children in the school she'd brought killers
to, as if she could murder herself and her lover while they
were still children. All of my rage had been left behind, with
the photographs I'd deliberately left on the shelves, let them
burn, let it end, let nothing be born from this explosion.

A flock of birds flew up suddenly from behind the car
and spread out and briefly netted the sky.

PART THREE

I opened the door, reached for the light switch, then stopped
as if my hand had been grabbed. The moonlight coming
through the patio door slowly drew the details of the room.
She was sitting motionless in my chair, her face covered by
a keffiyeh. A poster of the enemy. I lowered my hand from
the switch, as though afraid if I turned the light on she'd be
gone. As my eyes adjusted I could make out piles of objects:
books, soccer trophies, my framed medals and architectural
awards, the samovar; she'd circled them around the chair,
the way we'd make forts when we were children. A picture
of her waiting for me in the museum at Achziv swam into
my mind: a human dot bunkered by the artifacts of the past.
Her hands lay on her lap, empty, motionless, weaponless.

"Look at you," she whispered.

I looked at her. I was fastened by the idea of her being
here; the normal, reasonable flow of time stopped, then
rushing to re-form around the physical fact of her in my
chair.

"Say something," she said.

But I didn't know what to say. Her eyes gleamed at me from the folds of the keffiyeh. I remembered the newspaper account of how the man in the apartment that the terrorists, that Maryam, had broken into had only opened the door a crack, a slit with her eyes gleaming through it. What was the etiquette, Deddy? Maryam nodded at me, as if acknowledging the lack of language to cover the situation.

"What are you going to do?" she asked.

"I don't know."

"I thought you'd kill me."

"I've thought of it."

"Why don't you?"

"I can't make anyone come alive again."

She nodded again. Our communication was occurring at a level under our words, informed by mutual experiences we didn't need to name: the communication of lovers made perverse.

"Listen to me," she said. "I need to tell you. Sometimes I forget you weren't with me . . . it's as if you were there." Cyprus, she said. Beirut and an apartment where she'd waited forever and a man in a green leisure suit. Her words spider-webbed into other words in my mind, stridently shouted slogans devoid of meaning and then images, faces corded with rage, the malicious laughter of strange children and then sheets of light wavering on the water, bodies spotted with coins of sunlight. Kfar Maya'an, she said. Her eyes were gleams in a slit of darkness. I reached over and turned on the light, and then I unwrapped the keffiyeh, feeling her sitting rigidly under my hands, a patient waiting for the results of the operation, but it was me who needed to see her face, to search it as I once had for the similarities and differences of our flesh. She blinked at me, tired, her face haggard, but with no other changes mapped on her features, a Dachau

that sickened me with the untouched beauty of its countryside, with the absence of any scars on the landscape.

"Listen to me," I said harshly. "I was out at your house.
It's gone."

Her face twisted. "My mother . . ."

"She's all right."

Her eyes went dull again. "It's simply stone," she said.

I stared at her, looking for cracks, for chips in the stone.
Her body was rigid in the chair. Her side was stained red.

"You're bleeding."

"It's nothing."

I put my finger on her mouth as I had on Yael's, not
wanting to hear her speak. Wanting only to see her wounds.

He unwrapped me as he'd unwrapped my keffiyeh. I let him do what he wanted. My side looked to be peppered with splinters of rock. Ricochets, I thought, from the walls of the apartment building, from the stone of my house. There hadn't been much bleeding because the punctures had been sealed with dust. My flesh looked swollen and petrified, as if it had been turned to stone itself. He finished filling the bath and I got into the water. I watched his hands, soaking the sponge, passing it over my side, squeezing, the water turning red with the blood that my father had refused to see, but the Jewish woman had said it was all right, I was one of them, and led me away, back to the sanctuary of Israel. Red with the blood of my virginity that he refused to see. The mirror above the sink was misted by steam, hiding my image from him. The water a broken silver mirror shattered by his body. At Achziv he'd undressed first, but now he was over me and covered and I was naked. I felt an ache of resentment, still there in a hard, rolled-up ball under my heart in spite of everything, that I was naked to his mercy, mercy given only from a position of strength: it was the only way they could show mercy, with their own vulnerability hidden, clothed. The movements of his hands quickened, rubbing harder, moving to my breasts, my throat, lingering as if he'd read my thoughts, his lips a thin line, his face constricted with the same pinched anger that trembled in his hands.

I was under a blanket, on a bed in a small room with drawings of buildings taped to the wall. Flying buttresses and arches. His room. I pushed off the blanket. I was in one of his T-shirts. My side was clean and bandaged, cleansed of stone by this architect, standing with his back to me, adjusting his clothing like a character in a film who'd just had his evil way, this architect who'd shown me the strength built into the dome of my house, who used his knowledge of strength and cohesions to understand how solid objects were fragile, how they could fly apart. He turned and smiled at me.

"Good morning."

I sat up. "Have I been out that long?"

"You needed the rest." He finished buttoning his shirt. I felt a scramble of panic in my chest.

"Where are you going?"

"I have no food in the house."

I nodded. He'd go to his uncle. A sense of peace opened in me; it made me feel tired again, my body heavy.

"Don't worry," he said. "You'll be safe here—no one will think to look."

"I can't let you put yourself at risk."

"It doesn't matter. You're here already."

Meaning I'd implicated him already. Yet it didn't matter. He'd leave me and go to the police and he wouldn't have to be here when they came; he wouldn't have to meet my eyes and I wouldn't have to meet his. I was already in jail, the last in a series of cool, white rooms. It didn't matter, I wanted to tell him, he could call from here; he could do whatever he wanted as long as he didn't leave me alone again.

"Don't go," I said.

"Didn't I tell you you'd be all right here?" he said, as if his words were stronger than the world.

I didn't take the Land-Rover. I needed to walk. But the idea
of Maryam waiting back in my apartment like a twin I kept
at home pulled me from the normal flow of the city; I felt
detached from the people around me, as if her crime had
grown from the joining of our flesh. In front of Mahane
Yehuda, dozens of stout, fierce women were trying to push
their way through the door of the number 6 bus. They held
baskets filled with the food they'd bought in the market
pressed tightly against their breasts and shoved each other
viciously, as if gaining the bus door meant a last chance for
the survival of their families. We shared a history and I understood them, but I felt no part of their struggle. Vendors
yelled prices at me, their voices as distant as if they were
behind glass. A man held up a coconut for me to admire.
Next to him, three beggars were sitting on the pavement
like a service of the city, their faces covered by black cloths.
A wartlike chin, sprouted with white bristles, sprouted itself
from the bottom of one cloth. I reached into my pocket and
gave them whatever coins I had. The one with the exposed

chin exposed the rest of his face and smiled at me, his ruined flesh caving in around a rotten soft wound of a mouth. "May the Lord cause His countenance to shine upon you," he said, like a curse, and I admitted to myself where I was walking.

The onion-domed church in the courtyard of the Russian Compound stood like a bewildered prisoner in his own house: an old Slavic peasant who'd awakened one morning to find walls built around him and his yard overrun with jabbering, Semitic strangers. Several Arab women were lined up outside the entrance to the jail block, each carrying a parcel of food and a carton of cigarettes. Jewish visitors with identical burdens under their arms stood in a separate line. Across from the jail, in the headquarters building, I could see the windows of my uncle's office. Inside would be his large steel desk and bulky green file cabinets, the same furniture he'd had since I was a boy, and no pictures on the walls and no family photos on the desk either. "We have to share you, your father and I," he'd once said, and I'd run home crying, picturing a Solomon's decision, a baby split by a sword.

For a second I thought I saw a shadow or a movement in his window, as if he were watching, willing me to come to him, to confess and be forgiven, to be split from her, and I felt strongly the pull in myself that had drawn me here to turn Maryam in, to disconnect myself from her. I hated what she'd allowed herself to do, and there was no symmetry in our crimes. But I knew it was useless. We were connected, entwined with echoes, with smoke made of the dissolution of the stone that had grown living into our lives and the flesh that had grown living into the stone, a fibering that would unravel to the center of myself if I tried to break it.

When I stepped away from the building, I crossed a border and none of it belonged to me anymore and I saw it, as if for the first time, as a poster of sunflowers and dancers. I walked as if Maryam was in me and I was seeing the city through her eyes, with the freedom of a terrorist.

And I had a border to walk over. Jaffa Gate was crowded with Arabs and Jews in their costumes. Shoeshine men knelt before the golden pedestals of their stands, and porters in sheepskin vests balanced great loads that hung from thin straps around their foreheads. A black flock of Hasidim passed me, and then a rush of young religious couples in skullcaps and shawls, pushing black baby carriages, going to the Wall. I felt a need to go along with them that was as strong and senseless as the need for love, and with it, its echo, the ache of loss, the phantom pain that Deddy felt from his missing limb. An army patrol wove a green thread among the dark-clad couples, pushing through in the opposite direction. In front of a café across from the inside of the gate, a cluster of Arab youths glared at the soldiers. I listened to an earnest Arab student explain it all to a group of Scandinavian tourists, then watched them all turn in unison to join the youths in glaring.

I followed the couples, down past the Armenian Quarter and past the reconstructed Jewish Quarter and the Wall appeared. I took a cardboard skullcap from the box in front of the men's entrance, and, holding it awkwardly on my head with one hand, tried to push into the mass of people. Birds were stitching back and forth overhead, caught up in a strange excitement. The group of black-robed Hasidim circled their saint, an old man with parchment skin and a candelabra of veins standing out on his forehead. Near them, some Yemenites, their prayer shawls pulled up over their heads like keffiyehs, were chanting their prayers in a drawn-out, panicky desert wail. One man, his sleeves rolled up on brown, heavy arms, had picked up his son and was holding him like an offering. I wandered like a nomad around the borders of the groups, the dancers before the stones, and then I understood why I'd come here, what these stones were, and I brought her with me, and the two of us rested our foreheads against the indifferent peace of the cool stone, against the remaining Wall of a house destroyed by fire.

. . . . MARYAM

My face waited for me in the bathroom mirror and he'd
taken the keffiyeh, so I sat still, in his chair. Hannah Brenner
was still staring at me, a slight smile twisting her lips. What
are you doing here, little Arab? What do you want with my
son? Haven't you done enough damage to this house? You
café intellectual, you cognoscenti, you crazy kid with an idea
that you had to try out on us.

Who asked you? And who are you to talk about damage
to houses? Why didn't you just stay where you were, what
would the difference be? You'd be dead anyway, framed on
some Polish parlor wall, surrounded by bookcases filled with
books about Jews, and the hills would be clean and wind-
swept and green with no white town on their sides and no
underwear flapping in the breeze against the side of a building and no appliance store with discounts for new immigrants or sick fund clinics or a characterless white block of
an apartment building with noisy slat blinds, no vulgarity to
erase from the landscape. Just the hills I'd run in, alone, my
feet finding the flat surface of stones as if I'd grown from

those stones. And what do you know about houses? Do you know what it is to us here, a house? Houses built like little fortresses, their courtyards hearts in their centers, protected by thick walls, cool, private, untouchable, their outsides indifferent shrugs to the world. And he inserts his explosives into that secret privacy because he's the outsider, the little naked floating refugee, and he wants and needs to come inside but he can do it only by destroying the outside and that's what his explosions are and now mine too.

And you're right, I need to take my feet and get out of here because now I'm the explosion waiting within these walls, but when I go to the door a weakness keeps me here, drains the strength from my hand and body and I can't go out. I'm in his walls, surrounded by whiteness, and maybe he'll keep me a prisoner here, become my jailer and his own in these silent white rooms with their so easily violated air of fragile civilization. He'll keep me, his very own Arab, until I'm an ancient, white-haired crone, shuffling around in a stained robe, quite mad. We'll breathe in our atmosphere, the poisonous vapors of dead houses and the dead rotting in the walls, until we both grow old and terrible, until we both grow into our images in the mirror.

Bashir kept an office above a candle shop on Christian Quarter Road, a small hidey-hole, its walls decorated with posters of movie gangsters: Bogart, Lorre, Raft, and Robinson. He curled his lip at me, a movie gangster himself. The sneer was like a secret signal between us, as if to say he knew that I knew the parody of the room was deliberate. Bashir the trickster.

"Why do you come here?" he asked. "I've told you not to. If you want more, you only have to call."

"I hear you bring it over the border," I said.

He stared at me, his eyes bright, then completed the script, like an acknowledgment of the unpaid debt he owed me. "I'm the hippie peace plan, right? But I only work for the movies, my life isn't a film. And right now I'm very busy, Ezra—what can I do for you?"

"I want to get someone to the other side of the river," I said.

For a moment, he said nothing. When he spoke again, he spoke more slowly, as if he needed the time to redefine me.

"Now you confuse me with the man the film's about—
Moshe Rabbenue, Moses our father. If you want to take
someone across the water, that's who you should go to."

"He doesn't have your connections."

"Ezra, I don't have my connections."

His eyes were locked with mine, a line of perspiration on
his forehead. He understood everything.

"You're mad," he said.

"So it's possible."

"Anything is possible—it's an age of miracles. Ezra, how
do you see it?"

I told him. For a moment he was silent and then he
laughed. "Anything is possible," he said again. *"Inshallah."*

He touched his forehead, lips, chest.

"God willing," he said.

The pressing walls of the Souk, of Christian Quarter Road
closed around me warmly, like sanctuary. The narrow street
was thick with people, damp, intimate waves of heat baking
off them. I let myself be jostled and turned by a phalanx of
American Baptists determined to gain the Holy Sepulcher.
A Hasid stood out in the crowd. He caught my gaze and, as
if it had accelerated him, moved quickly down the street.

I walked slowly. The Hasid flitted after me, a shadow in
the corner of my eye, one of Naftali's avenging shadows; a
fanatic sent to nudj me in a nagging, wheedling voice about
an unpaid debt.

A mannequin begged at me suddenly from a shop window, sending a shock through me, heavy as liquid. I hadn't
thought it would happen this soon. But I knew who'd sent
this negative twin to follow me, halves drawn to each other
just the way my reflection moved now, superimposing itself

over the mannequin, the dummy behind the glass. I could see the reflection of the Hasid in the window too, a shadow flowing inexorably, joining and darkening the double image in front of my eyes.

I went up Frere's Road, a stepped street that rose at a steep angle. Halfway up it was a large arched door with a sign in Arabic and English above it: Arab Christian Boys' Club. I heard the faint clicking of pool balls and peals of laughter coming from farther inside, but the high-vaulted entrance hall was empty. I went into it and pressed myself against the inner wall, standing in a pool of shadow. I could just see the street. The echoing chant of a priest filled the cool passageway. The Hasid walked by quickly, my second twin from my other father.

I leaned against the stone wall, forcing myself to stop and think clearly. At least I was right about the apartment: they hadn't looked there. If they had, there'd be no need to follow me now. I'd expected to be followed: I knew Bashir was watched. But I was being boxed too closely now and I needed more room.

The small, plump policewoman behind the desk stared at me with wide, astonished eyes.

"Look, do you mind if I leave this here?" I put the plastic basket with the food I'd bought next to her desk.

"He told me nothing about an appointment."

"I don't have one. It's a family matter."

"Let me see your identification card."

I handed it to her. She put it on the desk and waited for it to speak. A man came into the room. He was short and blond and wore a white shirt and jeans. He didn't acknowledge me, but bent over and whispered in the policewoman's ear. She shrugged, as if dismissing the idiosyncrasies of her superiors and handed my card back to me. The man was staring at me.

"Do you know where to go?"

"Yes."

I went up a flight of stairs and down a long corridor to my uncle's office. Aharon stood up when I came in. His face trembled between an expression of grief and an expression of triumph, uncertain which was the appropriate emotion for my visit.

"Why are you here?"

"Why are your people following me?"

A fly made cryptic patterns in the air above Aharon's desk. Aharon stared at it a moment as if trying to break its code, then shrugged and spread his hands.

"Listen," I said. "I'll save you some trouble. I'm going down to Ein Duq for a few days—I'm working for Bashir Tawfik again. You can tell your people ahead of time, so they'll know where to go."

Aharon said nothing. He sat back down. The edge of his desk that faced me was worn and shiny as a coin, as if generations of prisoners had sat in front of it, running their thumbs nervously over the metal just as I'd done when I was a boy, waiting their turn for confession, for redemption.

"You could have asked for my cooperation," I said.

"Could I really?" Aharon raised his head slowly and stared at me. "Is it true?" he asked, like a child asking about God.

And the door opened. And the jailer came in.

He put down the shopping bag he was carrying, turned and locked the door, put on the chain. An elaborate pantomime, but for what purpose? He came over to the chair.

"Are you all right?"

I couldn't be better, dear. And how was your day?

He stroked my neck. "You must be hungry."

I followed him into the kitchen. He took a carton of eggs out of the bag and broke four of them into a frying pan. He brewed a pot of coffee. Brought bread to the table. Butter. Cheese. Yogurt. A bottle of juice. I stared at him.

"Set the table, would you?" he said.

I opened drawers and cupboards. Found place mats, plates, glasses, silverware, napkins. Put them down. Sat. Ezra brought the pan over and dumped two staring eggs, their edges bordered with black lace, onto my plate. I tested them with my fork.

"One of us will have to learn how to cook," he said.

Joking about the eggs. Chatting. A normal dinner in a

normal kitchen where you couldn't tell day from night. Like any young couple. White tile floors and framed prints on the walls and a murderer at the table. Arabs and Jews and cakes and grapefruit juice. He touched my face.

"I'm going to leave," I said.

He smiled. "You're always leaving."

"And for the same reason. I still don't have a country to give up for you. This house isn't my country—I don't want your forgiveness or your sanctuary: who are you to give me either?"

"I can't give you either," he said.

"Ezra, there's nothing we can do."

"There's something we can do," he said.

He told me what it was.

I stared at him.

"Will Bashir take us to the promised land, signal us ashore, then let us wander different deserts until we're worthy, all our sins forgiven?"

"Something like that."

"Why are you doing this?"

He shrugged. "Maybe because I have a country to give up for you."

"Shit. I won't live on your mercy. And I won't involve you any more than I already have. Ezra, I was crazy when I came here."

"I'm involved in you. Do you understand that?"

"No. It's insane too."

He shrugged again. "Being here with you is the first time I've felt sane since you left."

I felt something tear in my chest like wet paper. It was that simple. We were past poetry and mercy. In the fragile silence suddenly holding us, an image from Achziv gathered for me, moonlight metaling a sea that contained no refuge, an alien sea whose surface he shattered and was born naked from and brought me into with him and out of with him.

"I know," I whispered. "That's exactly how I feel. But that's insane too. Listen to me. What happened at Kfar Maya'an was impossible, but once I saw it, it became possible. It became possible in me. Can you still want to come inside me, into that?"

"Who else?"

He leaned over and pushed my hair up and kissed the back of my neck. I stood up, cleaved myself to him, pushing against him blindly. The hunger I felt shook me—it was a force that had lived in me like a stranger. Like a hope. He took me to his room. We undressed each other as if we were unwrapping presents. He kissed my breasts, belly, then down into the shadows of me. I wanted to take him into my mouth; when I did he turned his face to the wall and groaned and I felt a thrill of power. I was in a place where everything was known and forgiven, in my husband's room; we could do anything we wanted here. I held him in my hand and put him inside me, better than death. But his thrusts burned me. I closed my eyes and saw a face explode, rip off, come flapping toward me like a bat. I held on to him for my life, trying to concentrate myself in the center of my body where he was, rebuild around that core. Felt myself shudder. Pleasure sharp as a knife. Felt wonder that I could still have this. That everything could live in me together.

She had gripped my arm, and even in sleep her fingers hadn't loosened. I could feel the time pulsing away, measured out by the even touch of her breath against my side. The curve of her hip rose smoothly from the bunched and shadowed sheets, the lines of her body suggesting escape. Smooth rolls of rock splaying down, notched by the highway, then continuing on the other side until they crinkled up into the bluffs and gullies that marked the drop to the Jordan's bed. Bashir's crossing point. I remembered the way he'd traced his finger along the map, a rabbi tracing the holy words on a scroll, touching lightly, past Jericho, past the turn for the Allenby Bridge, past the oasis at Ein Duq where once Deddy and I had waited before we were rushed to the Golan during those first days when everyone was afraid that the Jordanians would invade and we'd cut out cardboard silhouettes of tanks and attached them to our cars and driven them back and forth on the road at dusk, to fool the enemy into thinking we were stronger than we were. Diversions. Deceiver's country. The long, crooked finger of a narrow wadi twisting

north-south off the east-west crack of Wadi Kelt, more or
less parallel to the highway, the border.

I traced the line of her hip.

The telephone rang.

I picked it up. When I put the receiver down again, Maryam's eyes were open.

"Bashir?"

"Yes."

"Can you trust him?"

His voice still echoed in my mind, from the phone, from
the conversation with him in his office that had been running
through my half-awake thoughts when he'd called. Ezra,
how do you see it? Like this: I'm going to meet her there.
I'll get word to her. But you don't know how we communi-
cate, I'd said, and his eyes had gleamed with what I'd chosen to see as intelligence and understanding.

"We don't have a choice," I said. "Even if I got you to
the border and over by yourself, you'd still get shot by Hus-
sein's Bedouins. Shot if you're lucky. Bashir has people on
the other side who travel back and forth like salesmen. His
man will get you to Amman."

"And you? I need to know you'll be all right."

"I'll be fine. We'll live happily ever after."

"In love's happy kingdom," she said.

"You claim Jordanian citizenship. You get a passport,
meet me in Cyprus."

The lie came easily. It was only another diversion.

Maryam ran her fingers lightly over my skin, memorizing.

"Love's happy kingdom," she said again.

I felt myself tugging erect and rolled away. It would only
be a diversion too and there was too much grief at the center
of the feeling, the knowledge of a last time. I felt her eyes

burning into my back as I went over to the armoire. My reserve equipment was in the bottom drawer: four canteens, my army pack, a sleeping roll. I put the roll inside the pack, then filled the canteens in the bathroom and put them in as well. The Uzi that was still in the drawer had been my weapon in my first war, a gun I'd fired in the streets of this city, in a battle I'd fought to erase the borders of my childhood. I took it out. Maryam was still staring at me. I tried to give her a reassuring smile.

"I don't even have the bullets for it."

"Then leave it. What do we need it for?"

"There'll be soldiers on the way down—it's part of my masquerade."

I had no reason, really, to take the weapon. But I couldn't imagine going into that country without it. I'd already crossed a border and it had become a strange country, an enemy country.

"Hurry and get dressed now. We need to get you in the car before sunrise."

She looked around with a kind of desperation, smoothing the sheets around herself, the copper of her skin against the white a picture I tried to fix in my mind.

"It seems like we just came here," she said. "But it's like leaving a life."

I busied myself, putting the weapon in the pack, tightening the straps. Then I dressed in an old set of fatigues and checked the house, turning off whatever lights were on. Aharon still might have someone watching the house, watching with a night scope from the field behind the building. But the Land-Rover was flush against the trees on the other side of the garden and it was the way I always parked and I could get Maryam into it low and he couldn't see through the car and if they knew she was here they'd have arrested us already. I'd gone through all of it before, but I needed to keep my mind working, keep it off where I was finally going.

Maryam was dressed. The act of putting on her clothing was like the final shutting of a door between us. I went out to check the patio. All of the neighbors' windows were dark and shuttered. I came back inside and put the pack on one shoulder.

"Are you ready?"

She slipped her hand into mine. I opened the patio door and we stepped outside and over another line and it was my house behind me now that had suddenly become a strange country.

Shalom, Uncle. We're leaving, to build and to be built. Shalom, peace be with you and thanks anyway but the baby did get split, split into twins by your bombs and my bombs and her bombs. They're our fucking poetry, those bombs, if you want to know the truth. And so shalom, and thanks for the opportunity to participate in history and all, but I'm leaving the planet for a while, Sergeant Architect checking out: the atmosphere is too heavy to build houses anyway; they keep falling down.

The Land-Rover was parked just past the line of trees, as if ready for escapes. I put her under the tarp in the back and we drove. Past Denmark Square, where we'd played house, down Herzl and right on Jaffa, past Mahane Yehuda and the absent crowds of people whose history I was cutting myself from, and past my uncle's cold castle in the Russian Compound, just like a film run in reverse. Then past the old border, the sun blazing suddenly, igniting the domes of the two big mosques, gold and silver, like promises of different heavens, and the small city of the Moslem cemetery like a dead twin outside the city wall, across from the desecrated Jewish cemetery on the Mount of Olives, the dead stirring, waiting the chance to rise and continue the fight, a flush of shame at the sight of the two of us, deserters from the final battle, spreading through the stones in the city wall.

I slipped us away, into the Kidron and onto the Jericho Road, then up and over the southern flank of the Mount of Olives into Bethany and around the sharp curve near the house where Lazarus rose from the dead. A flock of Arab schoolgirls, briefcases strapped to their backs, jumped out of my way at the last moment, laughing as if they knew the secret of resurrection. The road suddenly went into desert, and we went past the white cubes of Arab houses, problems in pressures per cubic centimeter, and then we passed a last house, lonely as a sentinel, and the bare stone hills seized the highway like a hostage that had wandered into its territory, and there were suddenly no more houses, no more crimes waiting to happen, only kilometers of clean rock, bare as a promise, smooth as rolls of skin, convoluted as a brain, the air above shimmering and stained with the baked-out color of the rocks. Great masses pushing together, shaping and folding to the blind needs of pressure. We rounded a curve and far below was the Dead Sea, cupped between its deeply riveted salt plain and the red mountains of Jordan, of Moab. There was an army camp near the side of the road, its tents bordered by white painted stones that tried to impose an order on the country. Two soldiers stood outside the border, pissing into the desert, creating their own order, and I felt the sharp sense I'd cut myself off from them, from the early-morning camps of soldiers.

"Are you all right?" I asked the empty backseat.

"Yes." Her voice was muffled. "Hot. Where are we?"

"Be very still."

There was a roadblock ahead. The soldiers looked at me

quickly and waved me through. Watch him, Aharon would say. But don't get too close. He's spooked already.

A Bedouin camp huddled at the base of a hill, its tents imposing no order, but black scrawls on the rocks that spelled out some secret code of the country. We sped down into the Rift, then north and through Jericho, yellow dust rising from the streets and the red flowers of the poinciana trees flickering like flames through it, and then we were passing the refugee camp where the film site had been, and the desert where I'd once imagined the extras fleeing was around us. To the right of the road, the terrain going down to the river was brown and flattened out, as if its edges were ironed down. To the left, bleached ridges and hills, cracked by shadows, marched to the horizon, to the Mount of Temptation.

There were two more roadblocks before the turn off to the Allenby Bridge. When we were through the second one, a dusty red Citroën came into my rearview mirror and stayed behind me until I stopped on the shoulder and let it go by, its rear window opaqued with swirls of dirt.

Don't get too close.

We passed Ein Duq. Deceiver's country. A wall of rock rose on my left, cutting off my view of the desert, and I pictured Bashir's finger on the map as on a holy scroll. Thus said Rabbi Bashir. Two point two kilometers. Just a little opening in the wadi wall. You can miss it easily.

I nearly missed it easily. I swung the wheel hard to the left, driving up between a gap in two loess formations, bulling the Land-Rover up a narrow ribbon of sand and loose rock that clutched my tires and released them like reluctant fingers.

Then turn north. Up the wadi bed. You know the area. You've trained there, Ezra. In your youth.

It's a good place.

It's been good for me.

I wove around tank traps, small concrete pyramids, like memorials to my youth. The abandoned tomb of a sheikh grew out of the left, western ridge, and I noticed that the wadi floor was sloping down. The highway and the border beyond it ran parallel to the wadi bed, on the other side of the rock wall to my right. We were invisible, two travelers in the hidden veins of the country, our route parallel but unseen.

Inshallah, Rabbi Bashir.

"Are you all right?" I asked the backseat. I adjusted the mirror until I could see her form, draped under the tarp, the twin I kept in the back.

"Yes." Her voice was fainter than before.

"Use the canteens. Don't hold back. It won't be long now."

"I'll be all right. Where are we going?"

Another three kilometers, Bashir had said. Then look for a formation of stones in the center of the wadi bed. Like some kind of beast. You can't miss it.

All the rocks looked the same. The odometer was past the distance. But it could be because of the twists of the wadi.

In the center of the bed were two formations that looked like the paws of a crouching lion, its body invisibly suggested. Across from the paws, a semicircle of tall stones pinched the air like swollen-tipped fingers.

I drove in among them, the Land-Rover barely fitting. I pressed the accelerator to the floor, ramming the vehicle in tightly, then shut off the engine and pulled the tarp off Maryam. Her face was very pale and her skin too dry.

"Drink some of this. Slowly, that's it."

"Where are we?"

"Off Wadi Kelt. Can you move?—I don't want to stay here too long."

"I'm fine."

We got out and pulled the tarp over the Land-Rover, then weighted it down with rocks. I walked directly over to the eastern wall. Bashir's path traced a faint silver zigzag up it. I slung the pack and we started up.

Near the top, I pressed my hand on her shoulder and we crawled the last few meters, into the depression Bashir had described. The small rock parapet that rimmed it cast a shadow. I took out my sleeping bag and unrolled it in the shadowed area. We'd have to wait here until dark, until Bashir came, and be as still as possible. Maryam sat on the unrolled bag, hugging her knees and squinting.

"Are you all right?"

"I'm trying to picture where we are."

Her calm curiosity was a relief. "Come, I'll show you."

We inched up to a point where we could stay in the shadow of the rim but still see beyond it. The rock beneath us sloped to the highway. On the other side of the road it bunched into long gulleys, marking the drop to the Jordan's bed. Copses of reeds grew in the gulleys. The river was invisible from where we were. The barbed wire that ran along it was invisible also. There isn't even a dirt-smoothed path by the river there, Bashir had said. The terrain doesn't allow it.

"Where will he take me across?" Maryam asked faintly.

It's directly across from you, he'd said. All you'll be able to see in the daylight is a green circle. That's what shows of a small jungle of reeds. They're very tall, two or three meters, so you can imagine how far down the level of the river is. The land has fallen beneath the fence there and I pay well to be sure it stays fallen. Orient on that.

"There's a place he uses about a kilometer from here. It's around the bend of the road. He'll meet us here, take you to it. Back down into the wadi, then over the wall again, across the highway. So, drink, rest. You'll need your strength."

I pressed her hair down on her head and neck. Her skin still felt hot, but she'd started sweating again. I gave her the canteen and watched her drink, her throat moving under a gleam of sweat.

I looked back in the direction of the border. I could see the road, the country down to the river, the red mountains of Jordan, pasted against the sky like cardboard cutouts, like diversions. It was the desert we'd march into, past the cameras and equipment, straight out of the movie, looking for the promised land. The land on both sides of the border looked flayed, ridged up in fleshy welts with pools of burning sunlight collected between them. I could make out signs of life on the other side of the border. Past the gullied wasteland near the river were fields and after them the tiny white houses of a town, spilled along the crests of some low, brown hills. A miniature tractor chugged back and forth in one of the fields, weaving the landscape together. The noise of its motor echoed faintly against the wall of rock, the key visual point we were on. This ridge at the edge of Asia.

Shalom, Uncle. We are leaving, to build and to be built. With songs in our hearts and trees in our hands. We're leaving. We'll uproot trees, turn farms into swamps, create deserts where cultivated land had been. Put the film into reverse. Forty years ago this was all settlements and houses, crimes waiting to happen, we'll say proudly.

A strong wind suddenly blew over the ridge, whistling down into the rock burrow where we nestled like two twins in a womb. It roared in my ears, then drifted down to a suggestive whisper, and when I tried to understand it, it grew loud again, like a frustrated man shouting his language at a foreigner.

. . . . AHARON

The wind parted and closed the reeds, revealing soldiers lying on their bellies, equipment. Like a curtain briefly parted
to reveal a play waiting to begin. Too much fucking drama,
the border police captain, a dark young man, had muttered.
Navon had agreed. We should have picked him up already,
Aharon. We know where she has to go. But we need to have
him in the act of being with her, Elhannan had said, smiling
pleasantly at me, and the captain had snorted. Then I was
mistaken, he'd said. I thought it was mainly the girl we
wanted. And Navon had stared at me. Enough, Aharon. And
what's this with the rifle? Enough drama.

But the drama is just beginning. Everything is in place.
Everything is where it has to be. The geography of the country is very clear and straightforward. One can see the logical
routes and strategies of all the armies that have ever moved
through it to take the city mapped out, drawn in its stone;
one can see easily the lesson of the desert, which starts at a
line outside Jerusalem, Starvation Line, on one side enough
rainfall for crops, civilization, on the other less and the bar-

barity of Asia. The country lays out its choices and one always suspects their simplicity, expects a diversion from some
deeper, more elusive meaning. There isn't one. What you see
is what you get. My nephew should have understood that.
I tried to teach him. I tried to teach him about Bashir. About
what must be done to live in the world and not be Bashir.
But he refused to listen. He put welts on my heart. Welts
like the configurations of the hills and valleys and plains that
hold and force time and action. The city and its country are
displayed, gridded, controlled by the iron logic of history
and geography. Two dots on the grid, moving inexorably
toward each other and me, both of them funneled by the
country. The dot of my nephew moving toward the dot of
Maryam Halim, converging as I once converged with the
dot of her mother, and then moving toward the dot, the
point in time and space that I am, all of us the living pattern
of an endless prayer, the physical representation of an elegant
symmetry that once achieved will restore balance to the
world.

The wind gusts down over me, making a soughing sound
in the reeds, a sound full of the memory of beaches and boats
and long nighttime waits. It's dark.

. . . . . . Maryam and Ezra

Bashir's face formed out of the darkness, his features cast dimly by the faint moonlight. A homunculus in the process of being created. Ezra born in the silver light coming off the sea.

"Is everything set?" Ezra asked.

"Say your good-byes now—we have to move quickly."

"How quickly?"

"Give me thirty minutes. They won't do anything before that."

I could barely see Ezra in the thick darkness. He was a shadow slipping away from me already.

"Thirty minutes," Bashir whispered, a password, some phrase in the secret language of shadows.

He tugged my arm. "Stay close. Be careful of loose stones going down, and be quiet. Can you do that?"

Come, girl. This time I'll take you over my border and no Riad and no airports and no Martians, we'll do it right this time, just like the movies. Come. Go. Stop. Go back and do it again.

He pulled at me, the whites of his eyes glinting in the starlight.

"Ezra, please—the timing."

"How can I rescue the girl," Ezra asked me, "if she won't follow the script?"

I could picture his smile in the dark.

"I don't know the script."

"If you go quickly, I'll see you very soon."

"Ezra."

"Go."

I glanced at my watch, then raised my eyes and waited a few minutes for my night vision to come back. When it did, I peered toward the river, trying to catch some hint of movement. There was nothing. I lay still for a long time before I let myself look at my watch again. Twelve minutes. They were down the inner slope by now, moving along the wadi bed. Almost to the point where they'd have to climb up it again, then down to the highway, the river, the grove of acacias Bashir had told me he used to mark his alternate crossing point. There were no noises, no sudden glints—no signs of ambush below me. The men waiting had to be border police, highly disciplined. Many of them Druze also. Like Bashir. Can you trust him? Maryam had asked. I trusted his laugh. His strange smile when I told him to go ahead, call Aharon and tell him how I was going to meet her. Tell him like you always do. Inform on the informer. I was my uncle's boy, I knew the price Bashir paid for his smuggler's freedom, but my uncle no longer noticed the outlaw dreams Bashir kept tacked above his head on his office wall.

How will it be, Ezra?

Like this. What you know is this. That I'm going to meet

her. Tomorrow night. At the point you gave me. Call him.
Tell him. As soon as I leave. Tell him. Just as you did in
Baka. What are you smiling about, trickster? Why are you
laughing? And, by the way, which way are you going, out
there in all that darkness?

A country of shadows. We move through them quickly and
noiselessly, as if we're shadows ourselves. Bashir ahead of
me, the back of his shirt a faint gray ghost. This strange
country. Rocks looming around us like pale mushrooms. The
moonlight creating a landscape of boulders and black-gouged
ravines. Cracks and crevices. The dim light making the
wrinkled landscape look alive, a creeping sentience—if I take
my eyes off it even for a second, it will flow into other
shapes. Ghosts gather round and tug at my shirt with fingers
of wind, whisper like wind rattling slat blinds. Shahid.
Come, little sister, no more games. The Bedouin are waiting
for us, dancing. Come and I'll protect you, shield you from
your own blood. Nu, little Arab, Hannah says. I take you
into the women's room and you bring me maniacs? Never
mind, daughter, the man in the green leisure suit says. Next
year in Jerusalem. This land was made for you and me. This
country of the insane. This country of shadows. Bashir and
I two shadows flowing through the rocks. A sudden level-
ness under my feet, so that I lurch like a sailor setting foot
on land. The road. It stretches on both sides of me. To my
right and around a curve, it connects me back to sanity, to
Ezra, up on his ridge, waiting his thirty minutes. What have
you learned? he asks.

    This, love. That I can't live on your mercy or even on
your love. But I can't live without mercy in myself. Where's

that leave me? Out in this desert. Saying next year in Jerusalem. Crawling.

Crawling like the training camp exercises I'd envisioned doing when I went to Lebanon. A game for children. I crawl after the shadow of Bashir into a black shadow, a crevice, a black crooked finger that points to the river, to the country where I can claim citizenship, get a passport, fly to love's happy kingdom by the sea. The moon is gone. I can sense the jagged stones around me more than see them. They're thickenings of the darkness, as I am. I am dark but comely, daughters of Jerusalem. More poetry. Stop. Stop here. The silhouette of a clump of trees, outlined in stars. A bush that doesn't burn, that sheds no light. The gurgle of water between us and the trees. The river. Beyond which I have a country to give up for you, my love. My sanity, back on your ridge, waiting your thirty minutes while I flowed from you like a shadow through this country of shadows.

I walk slowly. I'm the famous goat in the desert. Seven minutes to get down the slope. The road flat under my feet. Into the rough terrain on the other side. Orient on the circle of green reeds. You go and orient, in this dark. But I can hear the water. The stars are very close here and their stillness settles on me. On sergeant goat. But the sergeant has resigned. Where the fuck are they? Probably in those famous reeds. Lying along the sunken bank of the river. Waiting. Waiting for our famous meeting. That's where I would do it, if I were still a sergeant. So keep moving. Just keep moving in the direction of the water and don't let the country turn you. Be a good goat. And try to keep the drama to the minimum, sergeant. Let her go with no bundles, no baggage, no debts. She'll be gone by now or soon and won't hear any of it. If I will it, it won't be a dream. She won't hear that rustle, that whisper I hear now, the faint sound of metal hitting metal. Sounds of preparation. The main character enters.

"There," Bashir whispers. In front of me, in the center of the dark cluster of trees, two small circles of light blink. Once. Twice. A car on the other side. Or a Haganah signal, telling me it's safe to come, that refuge awaits me. Ezra is on his ridge behind me and I want to flow back to him, a shadow shrinking back to its source, but Bashir is urging me forward, telling me come on, move, and I come on and move, move toward the light and across the water and hands are helping me, pulling me as if from a womb.

A circle of blinding light explodes in my eyes. A dazzling whiteness. I spin toward a boulder to my right and yell, "Run, Maryam," just for the hell of it. My last diversion. "Over there," someone yells, seeing shadows. The light swings out of my eyes. A flare pops, then another. They drift down under their small parachutes, casting widening circles of greenish light that illuminate the toothy rocks, the dark reeds, the land in front of the river: Aharon's stage. But she'll be gone by now, moving through the magic of film past the cameras and equipment and past the border of the set.

Two white beams search back and forth over the ground to my left, like frantic fingers unsure where to point.

I step into my uncle's movie. The spotlights cross and find me again. I raise the empty Uzi at them, in the spirit of theater. The light flashes, goes through me like fire. I'm on the ground, the stars spinning. I try to get to my feet, but my right leg won't support me and I fall back to the rocks. I try again, performing, the lights on me. My leg burns. I hadn't heard the shot.

Soldiers rise in front of me, as if the reeds have been transformed. They are silhouetted by the light behind them, their helmeted heads looking grotesquely swollen. Clearly now, in the white bathing light, I see my uncle. He is rocking back and forth as if in mourning, a rifle cradled in his arms like his own dead child, but I can feel her gliding away and the sudden lightness of my own freedom, as if something has been born from me.